Olivia ha[illegible] such pleasur[illegible]altz before!

Captain Denning moved more gracefully than she could possibly have expected, but somehow she knew it was not just his dancing that was affecting her so powerfully that evening.

She raised her eyes, smiling a little shyly. Was it her imagination, or had some of the shadows lifted from his face? He seemed that night to have shed some of the strain which she had seen in him the morning they had met in his woods. Perhaps the sea air had begun to improve his health?

Jack smiled in return, and Olivia's heart did a rapid somersault. There was such charm and sweetness in his face at that moment, but also a haunting sadness. She wondered what lay behind his expression. What could possibly have caused so much pain?

A young woman disappears.
A husband is suspected of murder.
Stirring times for all the neighbourhood in

Book 9

When the debauched Marquis of Sywell won Steepwood Abbey years ago at cards, it led to the death of the then Earl of Yardley. Now he's caused scandal again by marrying a girl out of his class—and young enough to be his granddaughter! After being married only a short time, the Marchioness has disappeared, leaving no trace of her whereabouts. There is every expectation that yet more scandals will emerge, though no one yet knows just how shocking they will be.

The four villages surrounding the Steepwood Abbey estate are in turmoil, not only with the dire goings-on at the Abbey, but also with their own affairs. Each story in **The Steepwood Scandal** follows the mystery behind the disappearance of the young woman, and the individual romances of lovers connected in some way with the intrigue.

Regency Drama
intrigue, mischief...and marriage

COUNTERFEIT EARL

Anne Herries

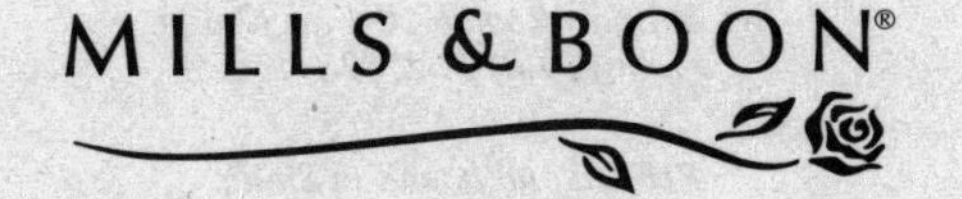

All the characters in this book have no existence outside the imagination of the author, and have no relation whatsoever to anyone bearing the same name or names. They are not even distantly inspired by any individual known or unknown to the author, and all the incidents are pure invention.

First published in Great Britain 2002
Harlequin Mills & Boon Limited,
Eton House, 18-24 Paradise Road, Richmond, Surrey TW9 1SR

Special thanks and acknowledgement are given to Anne Herries for her contribution to The Steepwood Scandal series.

ISBN 0 263 82850 6

Set in Times Roman 10½ on 12½ pt.
119-0102-57828

Printed and bound in Spain
by Litografia Rosés S.A., Barcelona

Anne Herries lives in Cambridge but spends part of the winter in Spain, where she and her husband stay in a pretty resort nestled amid the hills that run from Malaga to Gibraltar. Gazing over a sparkling blue ocean, watching the sunbeams dance like silver confetti on the restless waves, Anne loves to dream up her stories of laughter, tears and romantic lovers.

Counterfeit Earl features characters you will have already met in *Lord Ravensden's Marriage*, Anne Herries's previous novel in **The Steepwood Scandal**.

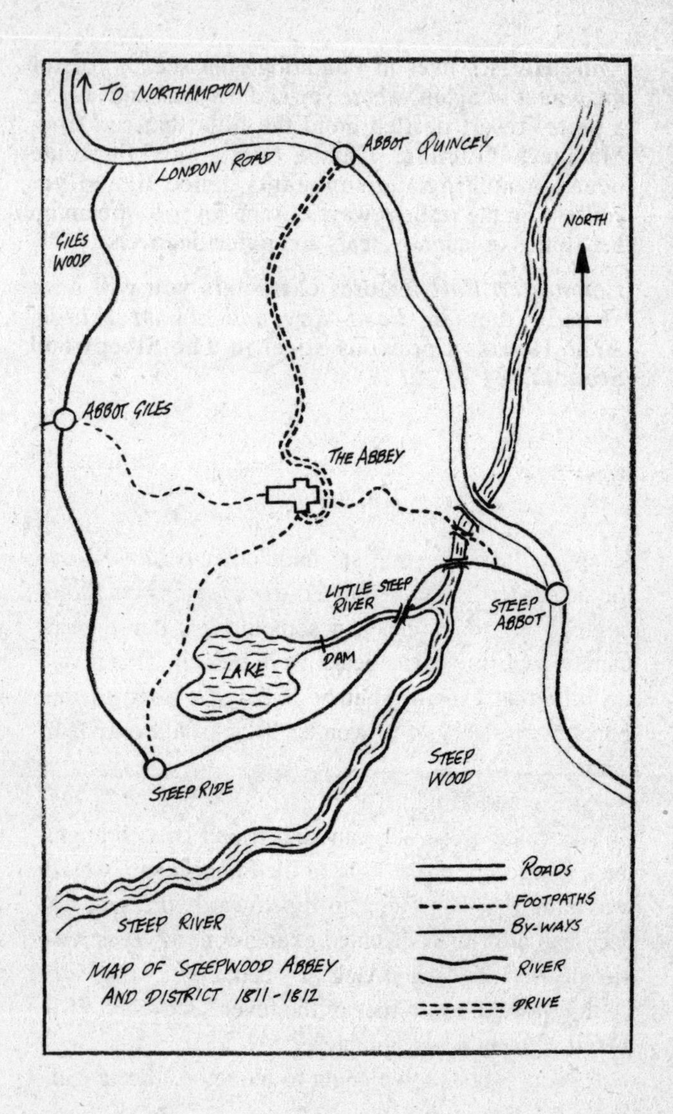
TO NORTHAMPTON
ABBOT QUINCEY
LONDON ROAD
NORTH
GILES WOOD
ABBOT GILES
THE ABBEY
LITTLE STEEP RIVER
STEEP ABBOT
DAM
LAKE
STEEP WOOD
STEEP RIDE
STEEP RIVER
ROADS
FOOTPATHS
BY-WAYS
RIVER
DRIVE
MAP OF STEEPWOOD ABBEY
AND DISTRICT 1811-1812

Chapter One

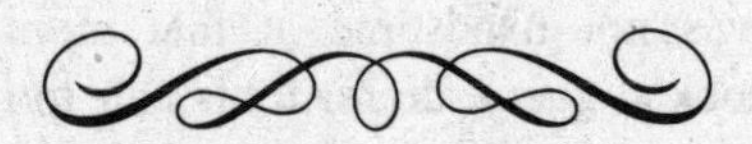

April 1812

Captain Jack Denning sat huddled into himself by the campfire. Even in summer, the evenings could be cold on the mountain, and sometimes a dense mist came down so that the peaks were hidden. There was no mist that evening, but he still felt chilled to the bone. He had begun to wonder if he would ever feel warm again.

'Still cold, Captain?'

The voice of his sergeant and friend Brett brought Jack's head up. In the light of the Spanish sun, which was only just beginning to dip towards the sea, his face had a tortured, haunted expression, his eyes red-rimmed by illness and lack of sleep.

'It's just the last throes of the fever,' Jack said. 'I'll be all right in a few minutes.'

'If you're rested, we ought to move on,' Brett said.

'We'll need to travel most of the night if we're to reach the ship before the tide changes in the morning.'

'Yes, I know. Get the wagons ready, Sergeant. I'll see to the fire.'

Jack rose to his feet as Brett walked away to follow his orders. He kicked the smouldering wood apart with the tip of his boot, a scowl on his once handsome face. It was not handsome at that moment. Jack Denning looked gaunt, drained, his hair too long and straggling in greasy disarray, a blood-stained bandage about his head giving him the appearance of a cut-throat pirate.

Damn it! That's what they all were, all Old Hooky's brave bully boys. Scum of the earth, that was what Viscount Arthur Wellington of Talevara, Commander-in-Chief of the British forces in the Peninsula, called them—and by heaven and hell, he was right!

'God forgive us all,' Jack muttered as he kicked earth over the ashes to dampen down the remaining heat. It would not do to have the fire flare up again after they moved on, there were too many enemies in these hills. That included the damned Spanish, whom they were supposed to be helping. Instead of being grateful for Wellington's superb tactics, which had led to success after success these past weeks, the pride of the Spanish generals had caused several setbacks and some of the guerrilla bands that roamed these hills would as lief attack the British as the French. 'And God damn us—you too, Wellington!'

It was twelve days now since the conquest of Badajoz, three since his commander had sent for him.

'I'm ordering you home, Denning. You will be in charge of the seriously wounded, men who will never fight again. It's your responsibility to get them down to the coast and on to a ship bound for England. And you are to go with them.'

'My wounds were superficial, sir. I was laid low by a fever for a few days, but I'll be fit for duty again soon. May I have your permission to return to my unit after I've seen the wounded safe?'

'Damn your eyes, sir! Do you not know an order when you hear one? The Regent himself has requested your return. You have done your share of fighting, Denning—at what cost to yourself we all know. I am recommending you for bravery in the face of the enemy…'

'In the face of the enemy?' Jack's brows rose.

'Yes, the enemy,' Wellington repeated. 'We both know what happened, Denning, and the consequences. With things difficult at home I am on a thin string here. I charge you to keep certain things to yourself. They will become known in due course, but I hope to brush over them…do you understand me?'

Jack inclined his head stiffly. 'I was never a gabble-monger, sir. I take no pride in what happened. Indeed, I shall bear the shame of it until my dying day.'

'Damn your eyes, Denning! You need have no shame.' Wellington scowled, his gaze narrowing fiercely as he inwardly cursed the fool who was compelling him to send this man home. Denning should have stayed to fight the remainder of the campaign. Only in the heat of battle might he learn to forget the horrors that were lurking in his haunted eyes. 'Do not imagine it was my idea to send you back. I understand the request came from the Earl of Heggan, and since it is a command from the Regent that I accede to that request, I can only obey.'

An immediate return to England was the only avenue open to Jack since his commander had given the order, but the resentment was eating at his guts as he turned away. Since he was ordered to return to England, he would do so, but nothing on this earth should make him return to that lonely, forlorn house in which he had been born. If the Earl of Heggan wished to speak to his grandson, he would have to come in search of him.

Jack had made a vow never to return to his father's house long ago, and he was determined to keep it!

'Is that a letter from Beatrice by any chance?' asked Mr Bertram Roade as he entered the parlour that afternoon in late June 1812 and discovered his youngest daughter frowning over her correspondence. 'What does your sister have to say, Olivia?'

'She writes to ask me to visit her,' replied Olivia, glancing up with a smile. She suspected that Papa was missing Beatrice more than he admitted. 'She and Harry are going to Brighton soon and would like me to accompany them.'

'Ah...' Mr Roades eyes gleamed behind his spectacles. 'I wonder if this would be a good time for me to begin my work at Camberwell? I have made excellent strides since I last spoke to Ravensden.'

'Bellows brought a letter for you, too, Papa,' Olivia said. 'It is there on the sideboard. I suspect that it may be from Lord Ravensden.'

'I shall read it immediately. Harry always writes such interesting letters. Excellent mind, excellent mind.'

Mr Roade pounced on the small packet with evident pleasure, smiled at his daughter and went off to his study, leaving Olivia in sole possession of the parlour.

She did not immediately return to her letter, laying it down on the little occasional table beside her, together with her embroidery and a book of poems she had been reading when their manservant brought the mail. Her sister's letter had made her restless.

Since Beatrice's marriage to Lord Ravensden six months earlier, she had written several times to ask Olivia to stay with her. Until now, Olivia had made various excuses, the most truthful that she felt she needed to spend a little time with her father and Aunt Nan.

Getting up from her seat, Olivia sighed and wandered over to the window to glance out at the view. Roade House was set on a little rise just at the outskirts of the village of Abbot Giles. On a clear summer afternoon like this one, she could see the church spire and some of the rooftops of the village houses…and in the distance the brooding presence of Steepwood Abbey.

How that place haunted her! There had been such shocking happenings at the Abbey these past months, culminating in the recent news that the Marquis had been brutally murdered in his bedchamber with his own razor.

A shudder ran through Olivia as she reflected on the strangeness of fate. Only a few months back, when she had first come to live with Beatrice and her father in Abbot Giles, they had all been agog at the news that the young Marchioness had disappeared. Olivia herself had been certain that Lady Sywell had been murdered by her brute of a husband, and despite all the rumours since, the most recent of which seemed to lay the blame for the Marquis's murder at his wife's door, she still wondered if Lady Sywell's body had been concealed somewhere in the grounds of the Abbey.

Olivia did not believe for one moment that the Marchioness was the murderer of her cruel husband. If the stories were to be believed, there had been a terrible fight, the Marquis having put up a struggle for his life. He had been a large man, built like a bull and strong. A woman would surely not have had the strength to overcome him.

No, Olivia thought, it could not have been his wife. Yet whoever had done it must have known the Abbey well. There had been wild rumours circulating in the village, but Olivia believed it must have been an itinerant journeyman or perhaps a servant who had been unfairly dismissed.

In the past few months there had been tales of a hoard of gold sovereigns allegedly stolen by the Marchioness in her flight from the dominance of her husband, though since the tale had apparently come from a laundress, who could know if it was true? And now the villages were reeling with the shocking news that Lord Sywell had been murdered on the evening of the 9th of June.

Naturally, no one had talked of anything else since. Despite the general dislike felt by local people, Lord Sywell was nevertheless a member of the aristocracy and there was bound to be a thorough investigation of the crime. Some people were saying that the Regent himself had ordered a report to be made directly to him.

Olivia had not been near the Abbey grounds since that terrible morning in November the previous year, when Sywell had threatened her sister with a blunderbuss. Although Lord Ravensden's brave action had diverted his attention, and Olivia's own actions had caused the Marquis's shots to go wide, they had resulted in Harry falling from his horse and so nearly ended in a tragedy. The whole affair had given Olivia an acute dislike of the place and its master, and these days she stayed well clear whenever she went walking.

Since her sister's wedding, she had been making

friends with various young women in the four villages. One of her particular friends was Lady Sophia, daughter of the Earl of Yardley, but Sophia had gone up to town earlier in the year and after a brilliant Season was engaged to be married. Robina Perceval, daughter of the vicar at Abbot Quincey, had also been in London. However, in the last letter Olivia had received from her, Robina had told her that she'd been invited to go down to Brighton.

Olivia sighed again. It was foolish of her to feel so low, but she could not help herself. Her life was so very different these days.

'Is something wrong?' asked Nan, coming in behind her. 'Why don't you go for a walk, Olivia? It is a pleasant afternoon, and you might meet someone.'

Olivia turned and smiled at her aunt. She was a pretty, delicate girl with fine dark brows, and her hair was a wonderful, honey blonde: an unusual combination, which always made people look at her a second time. Her eyes were blue, though at times they could take on a greenish tint, but it was when she smiled that her beauty really showed through.

'Is it so obvious that I am moping?' she asked, knowing that Nan did not have as much sympathy for her as her sister had always shown. 'I know I should not. It is just that I miss Beatrice.'

'You are not the only one in this house who misses her,' Nan said, and frowned. 'Why do you not go and stay with her? She has asked you often enough.'

'She has written to ask me to accompany her and

Harry to Brighton next month,' Olivia said, wrinkling her brow. 'Do you think I should go, Nan?'

'Most of your friends will be there,' Nan said. 'You will have to face up to it one day, Olivia. You cannot hide in this house for the rest of your life...unless you mean to go into a decline?'

'No, no, I do not mean to do that,' Olivia replied. 'And I am not afraid of facing people, Nan. Besides, Harry has told everyone that the talk of my having jilted him was simply a mistake, that we agreed to part on a mutual wish...because he had fallen in love with my sister. People may not believe it in their hearts but if he says it is so they will accept it, and of course no one will criticise him, because of who he is.'

'Money and power will sway most,' admitted her aunt. 'And you cannot blame people for being shocked, though I believe you did the right thing in the end. I am sorry the Burtons treated you so harshly, my dear. It was unkind of them to turn you out simply because you decided you did not wish to marry Lord Ravensden—but by staying here in obscurity, you are giving them best. Lord Ravensden settled a generous sum on you. Why don't you make some use of it? Show all the scandalmongers that you are more than a match for them!' She smiled at Olivia. 'I know you sometimes feel I am not as understanding as I might be, my dear, but it is only my way. I should like to see you happy, and that is something you are obviously not at this moment.'

'I have tried to be content here with you and Papa,' Olivia said, 'truly I have, Nan. It is just that almost everyone seems to be in town or at Brighton just now. I was always used to company, and I soon tire of sitting alone.'

'Not quite everyone,' her aunt said. 'I saw Annabel Lett in the village this morning. She asked me to remind you that you promised to walk over and take her a book of stories for her daughter.'

'Yes, so I did,' Olivia replied, brightening. 'Yes. I remember. It was a rather splendid picture book of fairy-tales that I was given as a child and brought with me. Thank you for reminding me, Nan. I shall put on my bonnet and go this instant.'

'That is a very good idea,' Nan said. 'And when you return, you may sit down and write to your sister—tell her that you would be very happy to accompany her to Brighton.'

'Yes,' Olivia said, and on impulse went to kiss her aunt's cheek. 'Thank you for your good advice, Nan. Perhaps a little scold was just what I needed. Papa is always so kind…'

'And so wrapped up in his work,' said her aunt. 'Neither he nor I are congenial company for a young lady like you, Olivia. We care for you, but we can only give you so much. Somehow, you have to make a life for yourself…and I do not believe that you find much pleasure in preserving or baking.'

Olivia laughed. 'If I could bake like Beatrice, I

might find it an absorbing task—but even Farmer Ekins's boy will not eat my cakes!'

'I dare say you could learn in time, but why should you? No, my dear. I believe you should go to Brighton with Beatrice and Lord Ravensden. Perhaps you may decide then precisely what it is you wish to do with your life.'

'It was kind of you to come all this way,' Annabel said, later that afternoon. 'Rebecca will enjoy listening to these stories—and the woodcuts will fascinate her. She has never seen anything like this book. Something like this would be too expensive for me to buy.'

The book contained several woodcut engravings of characters and scenes from the fairy-stories, some of which had been hand coloured. It was an expensive gift, one of many similar which had been lavished on Olivia as a child.

'I am pleased for her to have it,' Olivia replied, smiling. 'I spent many happy hours looking at it as a child. Is Rebecca in her crib?'

'Yes. I had just put her down when you arrived. She needs her afternoon nap.'

'Then we must not disturb her.'

'But you will stay for some tea before you go?'

'Thank you.' Olivia sat down. 'The news about Lord Sywell was shocking, was it not?'

'Yes, indeed.' Annabel shook her head. 'There are

so many stories going round that it is difficult to know what is true and what is false.'

'My aunt was told that he was completely...naked.'

'There are even more shocking stories,' said Annabel. 'I cannot bring myself to repeat most of them, nor do I believe they are true—but it seems that there must have been a terrible struggle.'

'Yes, so we were told.'

'Surely the murderer must have been covered in blood?'

Olivia shuddered. 'Pray do not! May we not speak of somcthing else?'

'Yes, of course. How does Lady Ravensden go on? Have you heard from her recently?'

'Bellows fetched a letter from the receiving office at Abbot Quincey earlier today. Beatrice is very well and very happy. She and Lord Ravensden are to visit Brighton next month, and they have asked me to go with them.'

'How lovely,' Annabel said. 'You are fortunate to have the opportunity, Olivia.'

'Yes, I am,' Olivia replied. 'Had Beatrice not fallen in love with Lord Ravensden, our lives would have been very different. We have more servants to look after the house, and we do not go short of anything. My sister and Lord Ravensden have been very generous.'

'Yes...' An odd expression crept into Annabel's eyes. She drummed her nails on the arm of her chair.

'Your sister was not expected to marry—to make such a match must have been beyond her dreams.'

'I believe Beatrice had no thought of marriage until she met Lord Ravensden. It was truly love at first sight in their case.'

Annabel nodded. Once again, her look struck Olivia as being wistful, even a little distracted, as though her mind were elsewhere. Perhaps she was thinking of the husband she had lost? They had never spoken of him, despite their growing friendship. Annabel did not seem to wish to discuss her past, and Olivia was too thoughtful to ask impertinent questions.

'Aunt Nan says I should go to Brighton,' Olivia said. 'She told me I must face the gossips. Of course she does not know how cruel some of the important hostesses can be. I dare say there will be some who will give me the cut direct.'

'But you will not care for them? Lady Ravensden must be received everywhere—do you not think most people will be prepared to forgive you?'

'Perhaps. I shall simply ignore those who do not,' Olivia said bravely. 'Now, tell me, what did you make of the Reverend Hartwell's sermon last Sunday?...'

Olivia was thoughtful as she walked home that evening. It was warm and pleasant as she skirted the walls of the Abbey grounds. How odd to think of it empty and deserted, except perhaps for Solomon Burneck. She supposed the Marquis's butler was still living there, that he would remain as a caretaker until the new owner arrived.

Who did the Abbey rightfully belong to now? Olivia did not know. Everyone had a different opinion as to what would happen to it, though she suspected that in their hearts most would like to see it return to the Yardley family.

Olivia knew much depended on whether or not an heir could be found, and since no one seemed to know if the Marquis of Sywell had any distant relatives, it was a matter for speculation, and would likely continue to be so for many months.

The fate of Steepwood Abbey did not, however, occupy her thoughts for long. What was she to do with her own life?

Since Lord Burton had banished her to the country, Olivia had refused to dwell on his unkindness. She had resolutely guarded against giving into self-pity, for there was no use in crying over something that was spoiled and could not be mended.

At first she had tried very hard to settle into the life at Abbot Giles. She had quickly grown fond of dear Papa, for who would not? She sensed that her aunt felt her lacking because she did not have Beatrice's skills in the stillroom and the kitchen, though she was not unkind, and they went on well enough together.

Olivia was not precisely unhappy, merely restless. She did not have enough to occupy her time now that there was no need for either her or Nan to do so many of the tasks that had been necessary when they had only Lily and Ida, and Bellows, of course.

Olivia had been educated as a lady. She had been taught to read and write and to calculate figures; she had studied a little history, a little art and music, and she was proficient at embroidery; she played the pianoforte and the harp, sang, and did a little sketching.

Perhaps if she had married a man with an important title, she would in time have become a brilliant society hostess, her drawing-room the meeting place for artists, poets and politicians. Olivia knew this was very unlikely now. She had jilted a man, an important man, and she did not expect to be given a second chance, since gentlemen did not like to be made fools of, and most would not care to risk a repeat of her disgraceful behaviour. Besides, she would only marry if she found a man she could love, who also loved her—as much as Harry Ravensden loved Beatrice.

So if she was not to marry, what was she to do with herself instead? She was an intelligent girl, and she knew her education was lacking. She did not know many things Beatrice had been taught, but then her sister had been educated at home by their father, who was an unusual man.

Olivia could study at home, of course, and indeed she had begun to borrow books from her father's library, books she would not have considered opening in the past. Although she was determined to improve her education through reading, she could not help feeling restless. She was in fact a very passionate girl and she needed an outlet for all the love that was inside her.

Olivia was very grateful to Harry Ravensden for settling ten thousand pounds on her. It meant that there was no hurry for her to make up her mind to do anything…and yet she longed for something to happen. If she had been born a man she might have taken up some sort of a profession, but very little was open to her as a female. She knew well that the life of a governess or a companion was a soulless existence, far less pleasant than her own at the moment.

'You are being missish,' Olivia scolded herself aloud. 'You lack for nothing…except perhaps a little excitement, a little romance.'

If only she were a man! She would instantly enlist in the army and go to fight with their brave men in the Peninsula.

The Regent's address to Parliament at the beginning of the year had mainly concerned Wellington's brilliant victories in Spain. One of his most recent at Badajoz had excited even Papa when he read of it in his newspapers.

'The siege of Badajoz has been attempted several times,' he had told Olivia, 'but our men did not have the besieging tools and battering rams necessary. However, this time, Wellington put his men out to sea from Lisbon and then went in secretly in small boats up the river to Alcácer do Sal, and after some fierce fighting the walls of Badajoz were breached. And Lord Wellington will not be content to stop there, believe me. He will sweep the French from Portugal and Spain before he is finished.'

Olivia had been impressed by the heroics of the men who had fought and won such victories. In her heart, she longed for adventure. How wonderful it must be to fight and win for the sake of glory and of England!

She sighed as she reached Roade House, knowing there was little likelihood of her ever leaving the shores of her homeland. The best she could hope for was to visit her sister and Lord Ravensden occasionally, and spend the rest of her time as usefully as she could at home with Papa and Nan.

'It seems unfair of us both to go and leave you here alone,' Olivia said as she kissed Nan's cheek just over a week later. 'Are you sure you will not change your mind and come with us? You know that Beatrice would be happy to see you.'

'I stayed with Beatrice for a few days at Easter,' Nan said. 'I am quite content here, Olivia. I shall begin preserving the soft fruits as soon as you and Bertram have gone.'

'And I shall be home within a week,' said Mr Roade, 'unless Ravensden wishes me to begin work on our project, of course—but I shall write and let you know. You will be comfortable here, sister. Besides, Olivia could not be expected to travel alone, even though Ravensden has sent his carriage and servants to fetch her.'

Olivia smiled at her father's thoughtfulness. After Lord Burton had thrown her out, she had travelled from London to Northampton by public coach, and from Northampton to Abbot Giles on a carter's wagon. No harm had come to her then, though she had been shaken until her body was aching all over, and her heart had felt as though it were breaking. However, her sister's kindness had soon restored her, and she was grateful now for her family's care of her.

'You spoil me, Papa,' she said, allowing Lord Ravensden's groom to hand her into the carriage. 'Perhaps we should go? Coachman will not want to keep his horses standing.'

'Yes, yes, no sense in waiting.' Mr Roade beamed at her. '*Au revoir*, Nan. I dare say I shall be back before you have had time to miss me.' He climbed inside the carriage to sit opposite his daughter. 'I must admit I am looking forward to seeing Beatrice and Ravensden. He tells me he has found the diagrams relating to the flying machine of which he wrote some months back. Yes, indeed. It should prove a most interesting visit!'

Olivia waved to her aunt from the carriage window. She found her father's preoccupation with his rather odd inventions a little disturbing. He had not yet installed another of his stoves at Roade House, though he had told her he was certain that the local blacksmith had not followed his instructions in making the previous design.

'It was the fault of inferior workmanship,' he said

now. 'I told Ravensden I suspected it, and he agreed. If he thinks it worth his while to let me experiment with my new designs, which I believe he must think exciting…we shall have the stoves for Camberwell forged at one of the new iron foundries. Then perhaps the workmanship will not let my designs down. I am sure that the principle is entirely sound.'

'Yes, Papa, I am sure you are right,' said Olivia, though she really did not comprehend more than a few words when he described his theories to her. 'For myself, I am simply looking forward to seeing Beatrice. It seems an age since we were together.'

'At last!' Beatrice cried as Olivia and Papa were shown into the parlour where she was sitting at a small writing-desk. She got up at once and came towards them, arms outstretched to embrace them both in turn. 'How glad I am to see you, Papa and my dear sister.'

'You look well, m'dear,' Mr Roade said. 'Blooming, I may say. Where is Ravensden? I am eager to see the drawings he wrote of.'

'He was called out on some business…' Beatrice began, but the sound of footsteps in the hall announced Harry's arrival. 'Ah, he is here now…'

There was another flurry of greetings, during which Harry kissed Olivia's cheek and shook hands with his father-in-law. After a few moments' brief conversation, the two men withdrew to Harry's library to study their papers, leaving Olivia and Beatrice together.

'Papa is right,' Olivia said. 'You do look very well, dearest.'

'I am,' Beatrice replied and embraced her again. 'Come and sit down with me, Olivia, and tell me all the news from home.'

'I told you in my last letter that Lady Sophia is engaged to be married, did I not? And about the terrible goings-on at the Abbey.'

'Yes.' Beatrice looked thoughtful. 'I cannot pretend to feel sorry that Lord Sywell met such an unpleasant end; one cannot but think he must have had many enemies...if all the stories about his disgraceful behaviour with the wives of tradesmen were true. I imagine there must have been quite a few husbands and sweethearts who would have liked to see him dead.'

'Yes, I suppose so,' Olivia said. 'People are suggesting that Lady Sywell might have done it herself, but I cannot believe it.'

'No, indeed,' Beatrice agreed at once. 'If she had wished to kill him, she would surely have done so when she ran away...if she did actually run away, that is.' She wrinkled her brow. 'I have always regretted that we were not able to finish our search of the grounds.'

'That was impossible after Lord Sywell threatened to shoot first you and then Harry.'

'Yes...' Beatrice shook her head. 'Enough of all this gloom and doom. It was really news of you I wanted to hear, Olivia. Have you made lots of new friends in the village? Are you happy and settled?'

'I have made friends,' Olivia said. 'I visited Annabel Lett a few days ago, and I went to see Amy Rushmere only yesterday morning. They both sent their regards to you. I think you are much missed in the villages, Beatrice.'

'I write to as many as I can,' Beatrice replied, smiling. 'But there is so little time. Harry and I travelled to Ravensden and to his estates in the north, and then we spent a few weeks in London… You ought to have come with us, Olivia. Several people inquired after you, dearest.'

Olivia blushed. 'Yes, I was sure some people would remain my friends.'

'Oh, I believe you will find that most are prepared to be kind in the circumstances,' Beatrice replied, a slight frown wrinkling her brow. 'I was told several times that Lord Burton was thought to be much at fault in his behaviour towards you. Indeed, Lady Burton has not been seen in town for months. I understand she has taken a house in Bath and sees only a few close friends.'

'Oh, poor Lady Burton,' cried Olivia, her sympathy aroused by this revelation. 'Indeed, it was not her fault. She was ordered to cut the connection with me, and had no choice but to obey.'

'I believe she may be suffering,' Beatrice said. 'If the chance arises, Olivia, you might want to try to heal the breach with her.'

'If...if she wishes it,' Olivia agreed. 'But I shall not beg for forgiveness, Beatrice. I believe that what I did was right—and you must agree.'

'Yes, of course I do,' Beatrice said. 'Harry says it was his fault entirely. He should have refused Lord Burton when he first suggested a marriage of convenience, but he was and is fond of you, dearest.'

'Yes, but he loves you,' Olivia said, and smiled at her. 'Had I married him and you and he had met at the wedding...'

'It would have been very different,' Beatrice said, then laughed as she saw the challenge in her sister's eyes. 'Well, I suppose we might have felt the same, but we would not have allowed ourselves to give into our feelings.'

'Nevertheless, it was as well that I jilted Harry, and that he chose to follow me to Abbot Giles—was it not?'

'I cannot disagree with that,' Beatrice said. 'Your bravery in standing firm against Lord Burton's threats has given me such happiness, Olivia. I can never thank you enough.' She leaned forward to kiss her sister. 'But now I want you to be happy.'

'I am happy to be here with you. I have missed you, Beatrice.'

'You know what I mean,' Beatrice said. 'Oh, Olivia, do not tell me that you do not wish to be married. If you could but know the joy of being truly loved! I know you would wish for it.'

'Yes, perhaps I should,' Olivia admitted as she saw

the way her sister's eyes shone with happiness. 'I fear I am too particular, Beatrice. Lord Ravensden was not the only gentleman to ask me to marry him. I did not like any of my suitors enough to contemplate marriage. Indeed, I would much prefer to continue as I am...'

'That is only because you have not met the right gentleman,' Beatrice said and smiled confidently. 'Believe me, dearest, when you fall in love, you will know...you will know the moment you look into his eyes.'

Chapter Two

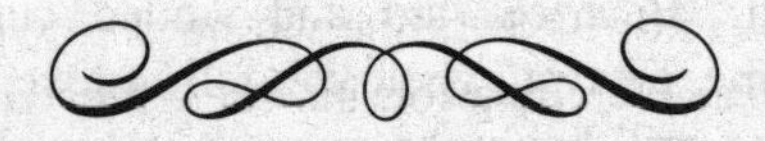

'Will you both forgive me if I do not accompany you to Brighton?' Harry looked from his wife to Olivia, an apologetic expression in his eyes. 'Papa and I have much to discuss, and I promise faithfully to join you in a week's time.'

'We can easily wait until you are ready to come with us,' Beatrice pointed out. 'We do not mind putting off our journey for a week.'

'No, I see no reason for you to be deprived of your pleasures,' Harry said, smiling at her. 'I had thought Papa and I would have settled our business by now, but there is so much to discuss. You will be quite safe, dearest. You will have servants enough to escort you on the road, and your maid, Beatrice. I am sure you and Olivia will find so many of your acquaintance in Brighton that you will hardly notice I am not there.'

'Was there ever such a provoking man?' Beatrice asked, and Olivia laughed. 'Very well, my lord. It shall be as you please. I should not wish to spoil your or Papa's fun. Olivia and I will go tomorrow as agreed, but we shall expect you early next week without fail—shall we not, Olivia?'

Olivia merely smiled at their banter. They were so obviously in love, but sometimes merciless in the way they teased each other. Olivia knew that such a relationship was not for her. She did not know precisely what she was searching for, but she believed the man she could love would be very different…more intense, heroic perhaps.

'Well, I shall leave you to tear my character to pieces in comfort,' Harry said with a wicked look for his wife. 'Papa has come up with the most ingenious design for a system of gravity heating, and we are about to inspect the east wing to see how it could best be implemented. It is really very exciting.'

Olivia raised her fine brows at her sister as he went out, leaving them in the sunny parlour, which overlooked a pretty rose garden and was Beatrice's favourite room in the house.

'How can you contemplate the idea of having your house disrupted, Beatrice?'

Beatrice smiled. 'We never use the east wing because it is so very cold. Papa can do no harm there. Besides, I have seen the new drawings. They look as if they might actually work. It is the principle of water finding its own level, you see. Harry explained it all to me. The idea is very much that used in those charming waterfalls you admire in landscaped gardens, where you see all the water tumbling down into a pool and wonder how it returns to the top to start falling again. The pressure of water carries it round and…'

'Oh, pray do not go on,' Olivia begged. 'I never understand more than a few words of Papa's theories.'

'That is because you have not had the benefit of Harry's explanations,' Beatrice replied, her eyes alight with laughter. 'We often discuss such things for hours at a time.'

'Truly?' Olivia looked at her in awe. 'How can you bear it?'

'I enjoy listening,' Beatrice explained. 'I have always been fascinated by the way other people's minds work. I suppose that is why I love to gossip.'

'Oh, gossip,' Olivia said and laughed. 'Now that is a very different matter, of course. Sophia wrote to me from town. Have you heard the latest about Caroline Lamb and Lord Byron? Truly, she is shameless! Everyone is talking about it…'

Olivia was thoughtful as she changed for dinner that evening. After spending a week at Camberwell, she could not doubt her sister's happiness. Beatrice no longer spent long hours in the kitchen cooking, nor did she clean, but her influence was everywhere in the house. It was evident that her servants respected her, and her household was impeccably run while retaining a warmth and charm that was often missing in large houses.

Olivia supposed that she might be happy in a house like Camberwell, which happened to be the smallest of Lord Ravensden's houses. Or she would be if she were married to a man she could love and admire; but somehow her rebellious spirit still craved adventure.

There was a strange restlessness inside her. She had begun to realise that her careful upbringing had been against her true nature. Lady Burton was a nervous, fussy woman, who had raised Olivia in her own image, but as each day passed the girl had gradually found her perception of the world and herself changing.

As yet she did not truly know the real Olivia. The girl who had loved to dance until dawn and flirt with the gentlemen who paid her pretty compliments was still there, of course, but she suspected there was another Olivia waiting to emerge.

'If only something exciting would happen,' she murmured to herself as she prepared to go downstairs and join her family at supper. 'If only I could fall in love the way Beatrice has...' She laughed at herself. At Brighton, she was likely to meet the same gentlemen she had known in London, none of whom had caught her interest.

'What are you waiting for, Olivia?' she asked her own reflection in the mirror. She shook her head at her own thoughts as the words of a poem came into her mind. A pale knight wandering lost and alone after the heat of battle...waiting to be brought back to life by a beautiful lady, who would take the shadows from his eyes… 'Where are you, my pale knight?'

Her head was full of romantic nonsense! Why could she not settle for someone kind and generous? Why must she always look for something more?

Dismissing her own longings as ridiculous, Olivia picked up her silk shawl and went downstairs to join the others.

Olivia sighed as she glanced out of the carriage window. They had been travelling for three days, having broken their journey by staying two nights with Lord and Lady Dawlish, who were great friends of Harry and Beatrice, in their house near the lovely, ancient village of Bletchingley in Surrey. It was now nearly noon, and they had set out at half-past the hour of eight that morning. They would soon be stopping to take refreshments and change the horses at the posting stage.

'Whoa! Whoa there!'

'What is happening?' Beatrice said, looking surprised as their coachman pulled the horses to a rather sudden and juddering halt. 'Can you see anything, Olivia?'

Olivia glanced out of the window. 'I believe there is an obstruction on the road. It looks as if someone's coach may have lost a wheel.'

'Oh, how unfortunate,' Beatrice said. She would have gone on, but her groom opened the carriage door and looked in. 'Yes, Dorkins? Has there been an accident?'

'I'm afraid so, milady. It means a delay while we help the gentleman to clear the road.'

'Then we may as well get down and stretch our legs,' Olivia said, giving her hand to the groom. 'Pray help me out, Dorkins. I need a little exercise.'

They had stopped on a quiet stretch of road, which was quite narrow and hemmed in by a thick wood to either side. One glance at the cumbersome coach ahead, which was tipped drunkenly forward, having lost its front nearside wheel, told Olivia that they would be delayed for several minutes while the grooms of both vehicles combined to move the coach off the road.

Beatrice looked out of the window as Olivia started to wander away. 'Where are you going, dearest?'

'Just to stretch my legs. Do not worry. I shall not go far.'

Olivia left the road, entering the wood. Her purpose was an indelicate subject, and one that she was not prepared to discuss in full hearing of the grooms, but she had been waiting to answer the call of nature for some while. She had preferred not to ask coachman to stop, thinking that they would soon reach the posting inn, but now she had determined to seize her chance to relieve herself.

Not for the first time in her life, Olivia found herself wishing she were a man as she gathered the voluminous skirts of her stylish travelling gown and squatted awkwardly behind a bush, which was well out of sight of the road. A few moments later, she emerged feeling more comfortable and began to rearrange her clothing, peering round at the back to make sure she was decent. Reassured, she was about to return to the road when she heard a low growling noise and turned to find her way blocked by a huge black dog. Its top lip was curled back over vicious-looking teeth, and it was snarling, poised as if preparing to leap at her if she dared to try passing it.

Olivia froze, unable to move so much as a finger. Her heart was beating wildly. She was terrified of large dogs. Lord Burton kept a pack of fierce guard dogs at his country estate, and she had once been bitten by one of them. The scar on her arm had almost completely faded, but the mental scar was still there.

'Do not move, ma'am!' a male voice suddenly commanded from behind her. 'He has been trained to attack intruders. Hold, Brutus! Lie down, sir!'

The dog seemed to hesitate, then it stopped growling and stretched down on the earth at Olivia's feet, its head on its paws. She tried to make herself walk past, but found she was quite unable to move.

'He won't hurt you now. It's perfectly safe.'

Olivia's mouth felt dry. 'I—I cannot…'

'You need not be afraid,' a voice beside her said, and then she felt the gentle touch of a hand on her arm. 'I shall not let him attack you. I give you my word.'

She turned her head to look at the man, her eyes

widening in surprise. At first sight, he was a little unnerving himself. His features were long, the chin square, rather thin, as if he had recently lost weight, and his dark eyes were red-rimmed. His hair was longer than was fashionable, very thick, dark and slightly curling, blown by the wind into a tangle about his face. His right temple bore a deep purple scar, which had begun to heal.

'Oh...' Her hand went to her breast as her heart thudded suddenly. He was a very large man, lean, but wiry, and simply dressed. She took him for a gamekeeper. 'Forgive me. I...'

'No, forgive us for frightening you,' Jack Denning said, his tone and manner seeming harsh though the words were kindly meant. 'Brutus was my grandfather's dog. Sir Joshua Chambers, the late owner of Briarwood—which is where you are. The dog was trained to keep gypsies from trespassing in the woods. He does not know that you are a lady, only that you are a stranger to him.'

'I—I am afraid I was trespassing,' Olivia said, finding her voice at last. So he was not the gamekeeper, but the grandson of a baronet! 'It was very wrong of me.'

Jack smiled, his features losing some of their harshness, becoming more like the man he had once been. 'I am Captain Jack Denning,' he said. 'My man told me there had been an accident on the road and I was on my way to investigate. Was it perhaps your own carriage, ma'am?'

'I am Miss Olivia Roade Burton.' Her head went up a little as her natural spirit reasserted itself. 'I am travelling to Brighton with my sister, Lady Ravensden, and our carriage has been delayed—the coach ahead of us has lost a wheel.'

'Yes, so I understand. I have already directed some of my men to assist in clearing the road. Perhaps by the time you reach your carriage, the way may be open.'

'Thank you. I shall go immediately.'

'You will allow me to accompany you.' Jack frowned. 'Although I believe you to be safe enough for the moment, I would not recommend wandering alone in strange woods, Miss Roade Burton. Were the gypsies I spoke of still here, I could not have been certain of your safety. They are wild, fierce creatures…and you are too young and vulnerable to be here alone.'

Olivia did not answer. For some unaccountable reason her heart was racing and she was finding it difficult to get her breath. Captain Denning had been kind enough, but his manner was not encouraging. She sensed that he was not pleased to find her in his woods.

'I…' It was too embarrassing! She could not explain her reason for leaving the road. 'I do not usually…'

He made no comment on her loss of words, merely cautioning the dog to stay before turning to lead her back towards the road. Olivia followed behind, feeling foolish.

She had never met anyone quite like him and she did wonder what had made that scar at his temple. He looked as though he might have been very ill quite recently, though she saw by his manner of striding through the woods that he had recovered his strength.

'Here we are, Miss Roade Burton. I believe your carriage is almost ready to leave.'

'Thank you.' Olivia glanced up as they both paused at the roadside, her eyes meeting his for one moment. Something seemed to flicker deep within his and for the briefest time she thought his expression seemed haunted, almost tortured. What could have caused him to look like that? Before she had time to think, the look had gone. 'Goodbye, Captain Denning. I thank you for your courtesy.'

'Goodbye, Miss Roade Burton. I wish you a safe journey onwards.'

'That is kind.' She smiled at him. 'Perhaps we shall meet if you come to Brighton.'

She blushed, wondering what had made her say such a thing. It would not be remarkable if he were to visit Brighton, since his estate was no more than twenty miles distant, yet her words were rather more familiar than Olivia would usually use in speaking to a stranger.

'I doubt that we shall,' Jack replied. His gaze narrowed, becoming colder to her way of thinking. 'I have no plans to visit Brighton at the moment.'

Olivia lowered her eyes. She felt as if he had given her a setdown, and knew that she had deserved it. Perhaps he imagined that she was setting her cap at him! It was her own fault. She had been forward, almost impertinent.

She walked away from him, her back very straight. What did it matter? She was sure she did not care whether he had thought her forward or not!

Beatrice was gazing out of the carriage window, looking anxious. She waved at her as she saw her, clearly relieved.

'Oh, there you are! I was just beginning to wonder if I should send someone to search for you, dearest.'

'I am sorry if I made you anxious. I went into the wood to—to, well, you know. There was a fierce dog. It snarled at me and would not let me pass. I dare not move in case it attacked me. Then a man came and called it off. I imagined at first that he was the game-keeper, but I believe he may own the estate. He…looked odd.'

'How?' Beatrice stared at her in surprise. 'I am not sure what you mean by odd?'

'I am not sure either,' Olivia said and laughed. 'Perhaps odd is the wrong word. Yes, interesting might be more appropriate. I think he had been ill. His face looked thin, almost gaunt, and his eyes…' She shook her head. It was his eyes that had affected her most. *'What ails thee, pale knight…?'*

'What was that you said?' Beatrice asked.

'Oh, I was thinking of a verse I once read,' Olivia

said. 'It was about a knight wandering in a daze from the field of battle...pale of face and red of eye...'

'Oh, poetry!' Beatrice said and smiled. 'What was his name, dearest? This man you met...'

'Denning...Captain Jack Denning.'

'Perhaps he was a soldier,' Beatrice said. 'He may have been wounded in the Peninsula, and sent home to recover.'

'Yes...' Olivia was much struck by this. She had been shaken by the incident with the dog, and then a little annoyed with her rescuer for implying that she was foolish to have wandered into the woods alone, and had not given his title much consideration. 'Yes, I think you may be right, Beatrice. That would account for his brusque manner. He did not strike me as someone accustomed to mixing in society often.'

'Are you saying he was not a gentleman?'

'No, of course not. He was definitely a gentleman, but his manner was a little harsh...or reserved might be a better word. I think he may well have been a soldier—and if he was wounded out there, it would account for his appearance.'

'Well, as long as he did not insult or harm you?'

'Oh, no,' Olivia said. 'Quite the opposite. He seemed most concerned that I was alone in the woods, and insisted on seeing me safe to the road. His dog has been trained to attack gypsies. Apparently they are a nuisance in these woods...'

Beatrice nodded. Obviously a country gentleman, she thought, perhaps with some recent military service. Olivia was used to the refined manners and gentle flirtation offered by the gentlemen she had met in London drawing-rooms. She might well find the abrupt way of speaking some country squires had a little harsh.

'It seems there was no harm done,' she said. 'Get into the coach now, my love. I think coachman is ready to go on.'

'Yes, of course,' Olivia said. She glanced back towards the wood but could see no sign of Captain Denning. Why should she want to? He was not handsome in a conventional way, nor charming. Yet there had been something about him. 'Yes, of course, we should go on…'

She climbed into the coach and settled her gown about her. It was most unlikely that she would ever meet Captain Denning again.

Jack Denning stood amongst the trees, watching as the carriage moved off. He whistled to Brutus, then turned to continue his walk through the woods of his estate. All the land to both sides of the main highway had belonged to his maternal grandfather until a few months ago, when the very desirable estate and substantial property elsewhere had passed to him through Sir Joshua's will.

Jack had been sad to learn of his grandfather's death on his return to England. Sir Joshua was the one person ever to have shown Jack true love and affection, and he had been very fond of him.

'Sir Joshua was a very wealthy man,' the solicitor had told Jack when he at last answered Trussell's repeated invitation to call at his offices. 'His fortune was made from trade, Captain Denning. Ships, coal and iron—he had invested in a new foundry just a few months before his final illness. I do not know whether you would wish to sell? I do have buyers interested, should you wish to dispose of one or all of Sir Joshua's assets.'

It was not usual for the aristocracy to be concerned in trade. Many young men in Captain Denning's position would have instantly sold the flourishing businesses and invested their money in land or the five percents.

'Not for the moment,' Jack said, surprising the lawyer. 'If Sir Joshua believed in them, I imagine they are good investments.'

'Your grandfather was an excellent businessman, sir.'

'Yes, I imagine he must have been. Tell his agents and managers to carry on as usual for the moment. I shall give myself time to think about the future before I do anything.'

Jack was not sure what he wished to do about any of the estate. There was sufficient money for him to live the life of a gentleman of leisure should he so wish, but he doubted it would suit him. He had loved the routine and bustle of army life—but that was over. His memories of comradeship had become tainted by those last hours at Badajoz.

He shut the pictures out of his mind resolutely. There were times now when he almost managed to forget…almost.

But there was no sense in remembering. He had failed, and his shame haunted him, most often at night when the dreams tortured him so that he woke sweating and crying out in pain and remorse.

He should have stopped it! Damn it! He should have done something. He had been so stunned, so disgusted by what he was seeing, that he had been slow to react…and then it had been too late. No, he could not go back, he must find a way to go forward, find a future for himself.

Jack frowned as he returned to the house at last and saw the old-fashioned, heavy travelling coach pulled up outside the front door of Briarwood House. The crest on the side panel would have told him who his visitor was had he needed to be told, which he did not. He had subconsciously been expecting this visitor for weeks, ever since his return to England.

'The Earl arrived half an hour since,' Jenkins told him as he entered the hall after scraping the mud from his boots outside the annexe door. 'I asked his lordship to wait in the library, sir, and I took him some of the good Madeira Sir Joshua laid down.'

'Thank you,' Jack said and smiled. 'You did exactly right.'

He glanced at himself in the mahogany-framed mirror in the main hall, brushing some debris from the sleeve of his coat. He was dressed in the simple garb of a country gentleman, but he must not appear careless. The Earl was a stickler for good manners, and it would not do to arrive looking as if he had come straight from the stables.

In the large, comfortable parlour, the Earl of Heggan was standing by the long French windows looking out on to the formal gardens. He was a tall man, silver-haired and impeccably dressed in knee-breeches and a frockcoat with wide tails, a style that had been fashionable some years back and was perhaps more formal than usual for the country. He turned as Jack entered, moving a little stiffly, his face showing no signs of the pain he suffered almost constantly.

Jack would not have expected anything else. Lord Heggan had never been known to show weakness of any kind.

'Forgive me for not being here to receive you,' Jack said. 'You sent no word of your intention to visit today.'

'I imagined you would be expecting me?' Lord Heggan's clipped tones spoke of his disapproval.

'Yes. I expected a visit at some time, though I was uncertain of precisely when you would come.'

'It would have done you more credit had you the courtesy to call on me, sir.'

'I believe you know my reason for not doing so,' Jack replied. They were very alike in that moment, two strong-willed, uncompromising men. 'You have been staying at Stanhope. I vowed never to return when I left six years ago, and I do not lightly break my vow.'

'You are a stubborn young fool,' the Earl said and sighed. 'You will forgive me if I sit down? I am past seventy and too old to stand for long. Besides, the journey tired me.'

Jack knew a moment of concern as he saw beneath the older man's mask and sensed how much of a strain he was under.

'Forgive me, sir. You are not well. I had not realized.'

'It is merely age,' the Earl said and frowned. 'I dare say there are less than five years left to me at most—that is why it is imperative that we talk.' He looked straight at his grandson. 'I know you have no love for Viscount Stanhope. I do not blame you. My son has lived as a wastrel, and will, I have no doubt, die with his sins upon him. He does not repent and swears he will not as he draws his last breath.'

'My father cursed me when I left his house,' Jack replied. 'I am aware that he is ill. Mama told me that he cannot live long when I called on her in London. If you have come to beg me to see Stanhope, you have wasted your time, sir. He would spit in my face and accuse me of having come to gloat at his deathbed.'

'I dare say you are right,' the Earl said. 'I am not such a fool as to waste my breath on a lost cause. It was my duty to see Stanhope. I have advised him to make his peace with God at last. I could do no less.'

Jack nodded. The Earl had seemed a distant figure when he was younger. Unbending, a stern disciplinarian who descended on the house only to make his displeasure known, but he was a just man by all accounts.

'No one could expect more, sir.' Jack looked him in the eyes. 'If it was not for my father's sake—why have you come?'

'To remind you of your duty to the family,' the Earl said. His faded blue eyes were seemingly without warmth or feeling. 'You have been sent back to England for one purpose. Since your father has only months—or weeks—to live, you must make sure of the succession. You must marry and get yourself an heir before it is too late.'

'I am seven-and-twenty, sir,' Jack said, a faint smile in his dark eyes. 'I do not think the case desperate just yet.'

'Your life has been in danger since you went to the Peninsula,' the Earl replied. 'Now that you have returned to England, you could be killed in a fall from your horse or take a fever and die of it in days. Until you have at least one son, there is a danger that the title will die with you. We have no male relatives. Therefore it is your duty to make sure of the succession.'

'I have no wish to disoblige you, sir,' Jack said, his mouth set hard. 'But at the moment I cannot promise to do as you ask. I have no desire to marry.'

'Your desires are of no importance.' The Earl

glared at him. 'I thought I had made myself plain. This is a matter of duty. Your own wishes are secondary. You owe this to me as the head of the family.'

'Forgive me, sir, but you do not know what you ask.'

'If you are thinking of love…'

'I was not,' Jack said. 'And I know what you were about to say—that I should make a marriage of convenience and take my pleasures where I will. You above anyone should know that the idea of such behaviour is abhorrent to me. I have a mistress who suits me well enough for the moment. She is a lady of good birth, married to a man who neglects her. Should I take a wife, Anne and I would part by mutual agreement and as friends.'

'At least you have some sense of decency, which is more than Stanhope ever did,' muttered the Earl, a grudging approval in his eyes. 'Why will you not do your duty, Jack?'

'If I were to marry, it would naturally be to a girl of good family, an innocent, respectable girl—and that I shall not do.' Jack's face was hard, his mouth set in a stubborn line. 'My hands are stained with the blood of innocents, sir. My touch would defile a decent girl.'

'Ridiculous!' snapped the Earl. 'You are a damned fool, Jack. I shall hear no more of this nonsense. If you wish to inherit my personal fortune as well as the Heggan estate and title, which is of course entailed, you will do as I ask.'

'Titles mean nothing to me,' Jack replied. 'As for money—Sir Joshua left me more money than I shall ever spend. I have ever lived by my own code of honour, and it is all I have left to me. Do not ask me to deny it for the sake of a fortune, for I shall not do so.'

'By God, sir!' The Earl's eyes glinted. 'If I were a younger man I should thrash you.'

Jack smiled oddly. 'You might try, sir—but if you were a younger man and not my grandfather, I might be forced to kill you.'

'Damn you! Where did you get your stubborn nature? Your father was a weakling, a drunken wastrel who gambled away his life and his fortune. Your mother a cold beauty with no heart.'

'Would you have me trapped into the same kind of marriage as they had?' Jack asked. Then, before the Earl could reply, 'And, since you ask, I believe I resemble you in character more than either of us had previously imagined.'

'Perhaps.' The Earl inclined his head stiffly, the faintest flicker of a smile in those faded eyes. Jack's remark seemed to have softened him. 'We should not quarrel, Denning. Is there nothing I can do to change your mind?'

'At this moment? Nothing.'

'Then I may as well go back to Stanhope. The servants will neglect your father if I am not there to remind them of their duty. I believe they hate him to a man.'

'Can you blame them?'

'No, I do not blame them, but I will not have him neglected. He shall die peacefully in his own bed, if not at peace with himself and his Maker.' For one brief moment there was a flicker of emotion in the Earl's eyes. 'I beg you, Jack. Find yourself a wife—not just for my sake, not just for duty, but for your own good. To live and die alone is a fate I would not wish on my worst enemy.'

Jack turned away, walking over to the window to gaze out at the sky, which was clouding over. For some reason he did not understand, a girl's innocent face had come into his mind.

'If I found a woman of the right birth, a woman who could bear me near her knowing what I feel, that I am tainted to the core and can never love her, then I might oblige you. I am not unaware of my duty to you, Grandfather.'

'I pray that you will find such a woman,' the Earl said. 'Indeed, you are often in my prayers, Jack. I sincerely hope that you will find peace soon.'

'Would that I could!' Jack muttered. He did not turn, for he knew that his face must reveal the inner torment he felt. 'Would that I could…'

Chapter Three

'It was so fortunate that we should meet like this,' Olivia said as she linked arms with her friend. 'Beatrice was feeling a little tired this morning, and begged me to take one of the maids with me on my walk rather than sit indoors on such a lovely day.'

'The Dowager Lady Exmouth felt exactly the same this morning,' Robina Perceval cried with a laugh. 'It is only to be expected in her case. We have been out until the early hours for several nights—but you arrived in Brighton only two days ago. I do hope Lady Ravensden is not unwell?'

'No, no, not at all,' Olivia replied. 'She is blooming. I have never seen her look so well. She was just a little sleepy this morning, but she assured me that she would accompany me to Lady Clements's ball this evening. I understand it is to be a rather grand affair?'

'Oh, yes. Lady Exmouth knows her well...' There

was a faint flush in Robina's cheeks. 'She has been very kind to me...Lady Exmouth, I mean.'

Olivia glanced at her companion. Robina had dark hair and blue eyes, and was quite lovely in her own quiet way. She had a modest manner and had not dressed to attract attention in the past, but seemed to have an air of fashion about her now; she certainly turned the heads of several gentlemen.

'You wrote to me that you had enjoyed your Season in London very much—but you did not form an attachment to anyone?'

'No...' Robina seemed to hesitate, then shook her head. 'No, I have not formed an attachment.' She sighed. 'Several gentleman were very kind to me, but I long for—for something different. A little excitement...romance.'

'Oh, you are so like me!' Olivia cried and laughed. 'I could have married...' She blushed. 'Oh, I did not mean that unfortunate business with Lord Ravensden...'

'Did you really jilt him, Olivia? People are saying it was as much his fault as yours.'

'In a way it was. I believed it was a love match, you see. I believed he was in love with me and—and I thought I would come to love him in time. When I realized that in fact he was marrying me to oblige Lord Burton, I immediately broke it off. After Lord Burton turned me out, Lord Ravensden came to Abbot Giles to ask me to reconsider—then he met Beatrice and they fell in love.'

'But he settled some money on you, did he not?'

'Yes, he has been very generous. I have ten thousand pounds, which is secured to me for life and mine to dispose of as I wish,' Olivia said. 'And he set the tale about that we had parted by mutual consent—which in the end was true. For neither of us wished to marry the other after he met my sister.'

'Well, it was fortunate that you did not,' Robina said, smiling at her. 'Now you are free to find someone you could love.'

'Yes…' Olivia sighed. 'I wish I could, but like you I long for romance.' She laughed. 'How foolish we are. We have read too many of Mrs Burney's novels. I dare say it would be most uncomfortable being married to a hero after all. He would forever be riding off to battle with dragons and the like, leaving his poor wife to cope with all the difficulties of running his estate and rearing his children.'

Robina nodded, but her expression was slightly dreamy. 'I dare say you are very right, but I would sacrifice a little comfort for the sake of true love, would you not?'

'I long to be truly loved,' Olivia said passionately. 'To be loved by one person to the exclusion of all others, to know that for one person you are the most important of all.' She blushed as she realised how much she had revealed of her inner self. 'Oh, I know that most girls of our class settle for much less, and I dare say I am asking for too much…' She gasped and stopped walking, clutching at her companion's arm.

'Is something wrong?' Robina followed the direction of Olivia's gaze. A man and a woman had stopped a few yards ahead of them on the promenade. They seemed to be looking out towards the sea at a ship in full sail, obviously admiring the view. 'Are you unwell?'

Olivia's cheeks had drained of colour. 'No,' she said. 'Only, may we please turn back now?'

'Yes, of course.' Robina looked at her curiously as they walked in the opposite direction. 'Did you know Lady Simmons?'

'No.' Olivia turned to her. 'Was that her name? She looked…remarkable.'

'She was a famous beauty a few years ago,' Robina said. 'They say she could have married a duke in her first season, but she chose a mere baronet. These days she lives mostly in Bath and apart from her husband, though I believe she visits him in town occasionally. She must have come to Brighton to see someone in particular, I would imagine.'

'Perhaps to meet her companion?' Olivia suggested, her cheeks pink.

'I wondered if the gentleman might be her lover; she has one, they say, but I do not know him,' Robina said. Her gaze narrowed as she looked at Olivia's expression. 'But you do, do you not?'

Olivia blushed. 'We have met briefly. On the road to Brighton. Our carriage was delayed and I went into the woods. His dog thought I was a gypsy and would not let me pass until he ordered it to lie down.'

'Then you know his name?' Robina was curious.

'Yes. He called himself Captain Jack Denning.' Olivia frowned. 'He looked as though he might have been ill and he was dressed very differently that day. At first I took him for a gamekeeper.'

'Oh, Olivia,' Robina cried with a delightful laugh. 'He did not look so today.'

'No...'

Olivia was thoughtful as she and her friend continued their walk along the promenade. There was no mistaking Captain Denning's quality that morning. He was dressed in a dark blue cloth coat which fitted him to perfection, showing that although lean, he was powerfully built. His immaculate buff-coloured breeches and highly polished boots, together with his exquisitely tied neckcloth, were evidence that when he chose he could rival for elegance any gentleman Olivia had met in London. And his hair had been trimmed, though he still wore it longer than most gentlemen of her acquaintance. It gave him a slightly rakish air.

'Were you aware that Captain Denning would be in Brighton?' Robina asked.

'No. Indeed, he said he had no intention of visiting in the near future.'

'How odd. I wonder why he lied?'

'I cannot imagine.' Olivia felt a little piqued. Surely there was no reason for Captain Denning to have lied to her? 'It is all of a piece with his behaviour that day. He was abrupt and harsh—and I did not care for him particularly.'

'Well, you will have to acknowledge him should you meet,' Robina said. 'But I dare say there will be no necessity to do more.'

'I am sure you are right,' Olivia agreed. 'Now, let us talk of something more agreeable. Beatrice was speaking of giving a dinner when Lord Ravensden arrives next week. Pray tell me, do you have an evening free of engagements?'

'I shall consult with Lady Exmouth,' Robina promised. 'But perhaps you and Lady Ravensden will call for tea this afternoon?'

'Oh, yes, I am sure Beatrice will agree.' Olivia smiled at her. 'I am so glad you came to Brighton, Robina. It is so much nicer to have at least one good friend one can talk to.'

'Someone to whom one can confide one's secrets,' Robina agreed.

Smiling at one another in perfect harmony, the two girls walked on. Both were completely unaware that a pair of dark eyes was following their progress as they crossed the road and disappeared around the corner of the street.

'Jack! You were not listening to one word I've just said,' Lady Simmons accused. 'Have you something on your mind?'

'Forgive me,' Jack apologised, his dark eyes focusing on her once more. 'I was not intending to ignore you.'

'You were just a little distracted,' she murmured, a sparkle of amusement in her soft grey eyes. She was a remarkably attractive woman, with dark brown hair and a wide, generous mouth. 'Tell me, which of the two young ladies drew your attention, my dear?'

'Was it so obvious?' Jack gave her a rueful smile. 'Two days ago Miss Olivia Roade Burton wandered into my woods. Brutus was preparing to attack her when I arrived on the scene. I was concerned that she had ventured so far into woods she did not know, for there has been trouble with gypsies, and I fear I may have been harsh with her. Indeed, since she could not bring herself to pass me just now, I believe I must have offended her.'

Anne nodded, her intelligent eyes thoughtful as they continued their walk along the marine parade. 'I know your manner can sometimes be a little abrupt. You must apologise next time you meet Miss Roade Burton, Jack.'

He shook his head at her. 'She is not for me, Anne. You know I have no thoughts of marriage.'

'I am aware that you have some foolish ideas in your head, my dear.' She smiled at him with affection. 'You are worth ten of most gentlemen I know. What happened at Badajoz was not your fault.'

'It is not just that—though it haunts my dreams,' Jack replied, his dark eyes shadowed with pain for a moment. 'I do not believe I am capable of loving,

Anne, not with my whole heart. Not as a woman I would make my wife has a right to expect. You are my friend. You do not ask for more than I can give.'

'I believe you have a great capacity for loving,' Anne replied, her look full of warmth. 'You were hurt too many times as a child, but one day you will discover your true self. Our arrangement has been a pleasant one for us both. However, should you wish to marry…'

'Yes, I know your mind,' Jack said. 'I have a true fondness for you, my dear. Had you been free, Anne, I believe we might have found happiness together.'

'Perhaps.' Her lovely eyes clouded with sadness. 'Unfortunately, I am not free.'

Jack touched her hand in sympathy. He knew that she was sometimes desperately unhappy, but her family would never permit her to divorce her husband. They had persuaded Sir Bernard Simmons to allow her to retire to Bath, to live quietly with a companion, but for the sake of the two sons of the marriage, the husband and wife met occasionally in society. Anne's sons were both boarders at an exclusive school, and she saw them two or three times a year. It was not an ideal situation for her, but it was the best she could expect. Her only alternative was to live abroad in exile, and then she would not have been allowed to see her sons until they reached their maturity.

'Do not pity me,' she said softly. 'I was deceived in the man I married, but I have learned to live with my mistakes. I have friends who care for me, and most of the time I am content.'

'I have never pitied you,' Jack replied honestly. 'I admire and respect you, Anne. You are one of the finest—and certainly the bravest—woman I have ever met.'

'One day you will meet a woman you can admire, respect and love,' Anne said. 'Because I care for you, my dear, I hope that day will come soon.'

Beatrice was sitting in the back parlour of the house in Royal Crescent; it was one of the fairly new houses built by J.B.Otto, an elegant three-storied building faced with black mathematical tiles. She glanced up with a smile as Olivia entered.

'Your walk has given you some colour,' she said. 'I am sorry I was so sleepy this morning. It is unlike me. I cannot imagine what was wrong with me.'

'As long as you are not ill?' Olivia was a little anxious. Having found her sister at last, after so many years spent apart, Beatrice had become doubly precious to her.

'Oh, no, not at all,' Beatrice replied. 'I feel wonderful. I hope your walk was not spoiled because I did not accompany you?'

'I missed you, of course I did—but it was the most fortunate thing,' Olivia replied, smiling at her. 'I met Robina Perceval. She was out walking with a maid, too. The Dowager Lady Exmouth was also feeling a little tired apparently. Robina asked if we would take tea with them this afternoon. I said yes. I hope that was all right?'

'Yes, of course,' Beatrice said. 'I met the Dowager when I was in London this spring. I liked her. I am very pleased you will have Robina for company. It is pleasant to have real friends.'

'Yes.' A shadow passed across Olivia's face. She had had so many friends in London, but she was not sure how many of them would want to know her now. 'Yes, it is pleasant to have real friends.'

'I have been reading some letters Harry sent on, which one of the maids fetched this morning from the receiving office,' Beatrice said. 'There was one from Amy Rushmere, who as you know lives in Abbot Giles, and another from my friend, Ghislaine de Champlain. Incidentally, she writes that she has found a gentleman she likes. A young curate who has taken an interest in her.'

'That is good news. I liked Ghislaine, though I saw very little of her. Was there any other news?'

'They both had gossip from the village to tell us.'

'Oh, what did they say?' Olivia was as curious as her sister to hear news from the villages. 'Does anyone know what is going to happen to Steepwood Abbey yet?'

'No, I do not believe so,' Beatrice said. 'Ghislaine told me there are many rumours flying around. Everyone is still wondering who could have killed Lord Sywell, of course.'

'Nothing has been discovered yet?'

'No, nothing certain. Ghislaine heard that a pedlar was seen entering the grounds the previous day, a man who was a stranger to the four villages.'

Olivia nodded. 'I am sure it must have been someone like that, or perhaps a jealous lover.'

'Yes, I dare say.' Beatrice looked thoughtful. 'Amy Rushmere's news was even more intriguing. She says that a rather peculiar little man has been to the village making enquiries about Athene Filmer of Datchet House—you remember that she and her mother Charlotte live in Steep Ride? And Amy says that although she did not realise it until later, he also prompted her to talk about Louise Hanslope...'

'I have seen Athene at the market in Abbot Quincey, I believe, though I have not passed more than a few words with her.' Olivia frowned. 'Was not Lady Sywell's name Hanslope before she married the Marquis?'

'Yes,' Beatrice agreed. 'You know her history as well as I, Olivia. Everyone imagined her to be Hanslope's by-blow—but it seems the investigator was very curious about how and when she was first brought to the villages as a child. What do you make of that? And why do you suppose he was enquiring about Athene Filmer?'

'I do not know.' Olivia frowned. 'It all sounds a little odd to me. Why should anyone be asking such questions...unless...' She looked at Beatrice. 'Do you think someone has discovered what happened to Lady Sywell?'

'Well, there must be some reason for the enquiry,' Beatrice said. 'Amy could not get any information out of the man who spoke to her, except that his name was Jackson—but she says she thinks he may be a Bow Street Runner. And a very clever man by the sound of him.'

'No! Then his enquiry may be official.' Olivia looked stunned. 'Why would an officer of the law be enquiring after Lady Sywell? Surely no one truly believes that she could have killed her husband?'

'I cannot believe that they should, but obviously someone is interested in finding out more about her,' Beatrice said. 'It is certainly intriguing, is it not?'

'Yes,' Olivia agreed. 'I do wish we could discover what has happened to her, don't you?'

'Well, perhaps we shall in time,' Beatrice said, and smiled at her. 'Now, tell me, dearest—which gown are you going to wear to Lady Clements's ball this evening? That pale lemon, which becomes you so well—or the white?'

The ball was already in full swing when the two sisters arrived at the large assembly rooms where the festivities were being held that evening. It was a glittering occasion, Lady Clements having given it to celebrate the engagement of her niece to Lord Manningtree, and everyone of note who was staying in Brighton had been invited.

'Ah, dear Lady Ravensden.' Their hostess greeted them with a beaming smile of approval and a kiss on the cheek for Beatrice. 'How pleasant it is to see you again—and you, Miss Roade Burton, of course.' Olivia could not but be aware of the slight look of disapproval in Lady Clements's eyes. However, she had been accepted on the surface and she knew it was up to her to put a brave face on the situation. She could not expect to be as popular or as universally approved as she had been during her Season.

She was looking extremely pretty that evening in a gown of pale lemon with a squared neckline, and a wide sash of a deeper yellow. Her hair had been drawn back off her face and held with a band of dark green velvet studded with diamante, and she wore a matching velvet ribbon around her throat with a tiny diamond and pearl drop that Beatrice had recently given her. Although so simply dressed, she was one of the most attractive ladies in the room, and heads turned as she walked by.

Whenever Olivia had attended a ball in London, gentlemen wanting to partner her had besieged her immediately she arrived. Although she almost at once saw several young gentlemen she knew well, they did not approach her, though one or two smiled in her direction. Olivia sat quietly with her sister, her head up as she tried not to look either upset or humiliated. It was all of twenty minutes before her hostess brought a gentleman to her.

'Miss Roade Burton,' Lady Clements said with a simpering smile. 'Will you allow me to introduce my nephew to you. Mr Reginald Smythe—Miss Roade Burton.'

'M-miss Roade Burton,' stammered the rather spotty-faced young man. 'W-would you do me the honour of s-standing up with me for the next dance?'

Olivia's card would usually have been full long before an immature youth could get near enough to ask her. However, that evening she was grateful for his offer, so she smiled and thanked him.

Since the dance being performed next was the first of a set of country dances, Olivia was not forced to stay with her partner the whole time. Which was fortunate, since Mr Reginald Smythe had no more than half a dozen words to say for himself.

As Olivia progressed down the line, she found herself dancing with several gentlemen she had known in London. One or two of them seemed embarrassed, but three smiled at her and said they hoped she would save a dance for them later.

The ice having been broken, the three young men who had been particular friends of hers in town approached Olivia after the set had ended: Mr John Partridge, Sir George Vine, and Mr Henry Peterson. All of them filled in one space in her card, which still left a great many free—including the supper dance. This was something that had never happened to Olivia before. She had known her suitors to come almost to blows over the supper dance!

To be left sitting with the matrons for a large part of the evening was a humbling experience for a girl who had been all the rage for one heady Season. Olivia did join Robina and the Dowager Lady Exmouth for a while, and Lord Exmouth was kind enough to stand up with her, after a hint from Robina.

However, she was very much aware that her welcome in society that evening was less than warm. She was being tolerated because she was Lady Ravensden's sister, but she was not yet forgiven. It was with a sinking heart that she saw Mr Smythe making his way purposefully towards her just before the supper dance.

'Miss Roade Burton?' A pleasant female voice at her elbow made her look round. 'I am Lady Simmons. You do not know me, but my friend has had the honour of making your acquaintance.'

Olivia flushed as she saw that Lady Simmons was addressing her. 'Good evening, ma'am—Captain Denning.'

'Captain Denning has asked me to intercede for him,' Lady Simmons said. 'He wishes to dance. I do not waltz. Will you not take pity on him, Miss Roade Burton?'

Olivia's heart jerked oddly as she glanced towards him. 'Thank you, ma'am. I should like to dance.' Her eyes met Captain Denning's. 'If you truly wish to dance, sir?'

'I should be honoured, Miss Roade Burton.'

'Thank you.'

Olivia gave him her hand. Her heart was still behaving in a very odd way. She supposed it must be relief or gratitude at having been rescued from another dance with Mr Smythe.

'I believe I owe you an apology,' Jack said as he led her towards the dance floor.

Olivia's startled eyes lifted to meet his. She was not sure whether it was his statement or the touch of his hand at her waist which had made her heart thump so wildly.

'I cannot imagine why you should think that, Captain Denning.'

'I have been told that my manner can sometimes seem harsh, even when it is not intended to be so,' he said. 'I thought perhaps I had given you a dislike of my company?'

'Oh, no!' Olivia's cheeks were burning. He must have noticed her turning away that morning on the seafront. 'It was foolish of me this morning. I was a little embarrassed.'

'When I told you I had no intention of visiting Brighton, I had none,' Jack explained as they began to glide around the dance floor. 'A friend of mine asked me to come for a particular reason.'

'Lady Simmons?' Olivia kept her eyes downcast, not daring to look up at him.

'Yes. She asked me to escort her on the road here, because she does not like to travel with her brother's children, who are rather noisy at times.' He hesitated, then: 'I am sure she would not mind my saying that her doctor advised some sea air. She has been unwell…'

'Oh, I am so sorry,' Olivia said at once. 'I do hope she will soon feel better.'

'I believe she already does. The visit is a means of lifting her spirits.'

Olivia nodded. She did not enquire further, for it would not have been good manners. Besides, she was feeling a little breathless.

She had never experienced such pleasure in dancing the waltz before! Captain Denning moved more gracefully than she could possibly have expected, but somehow she knew it was not just his dancing that was affecting her so powerfully that evening.

She raised her eyes, smiling a little shyly. Was it her imagination, or had some of the shadows lifted from his face? He seemed that night to have shed some of the strain which she had seen in him the morning they had met in his woods. Perhaps the sea air had begun to improve his health?

Jack smiled in return, and Olivia's heart did a rapid somersault. There was such charm and sweetness in his face at that moment, but also a haunting sadness. She wondered what lay behind his expression. What could possibly have caused him so much pain?

She wanted to reach up and touch his cheek, to ease away the hurt that was so obvious to her. Naturally she could do no such thing, and in another moment the smile and the sadness were gone, hidden beneath the stern expression he habitually assumed.

Olivia was not fooled. She had seen beneath the mask to the real man, and she sensed that his harsh manner was a kind of shield. Quite how she could know so much from one glance was not clear to her, but her instinct told her that she had somehow discovered the true man and she was intrigued.

This feeling of floating was heavenly. Oh, how she wished this dance might go on for ever!

She held her sigh of disappointment inside as the music ended.

'Will you do me the honour of taking supper with me?'

Olivia glanced up at Captain Denning as he led her from the floor. 'It is kind of you to ask, sir—but should you not return to Lady Simmons?'

'Anne is with her brother's party this evening,' Jack told her. 'She came to Brighton in their company, and is staying at Lord Wilburton's house.'

'Oh…' Olivia blushed. 'Then I should be much obliged, Captain Denning.'

He looked at her thoughtfully. 'Men are often fools, Miss Roade Burton. You must forgive us for much that we do.'

He had obviously heard the gossip about her, and he must have noticed her sitting out many of the dances earlier. Olivia's head went up proudly.

'I brought my situation on myself, sir. I discovered that I could not love Lord Ravensden. Nor did he truly love me. It would have been wrong for us both had I gone through with the marriage. I know what I did has offended many…'

'What you did was both brave and honest,' Jack

replied. 'I respect you for having the courage, Miss Roade Burton.'

Olivia smiled. 'I dare say you thought me a silly chit when I could not bring myself to walk past your dog the other day, but I was bitten quite badly as a child and I *am* frightened of dogs.'

'But of not much else, I think?'

His eyes quizzed her, and something in his tone made Olivia's heart race wildly. Really, what was the matter with her? She had never, ever felt like this before! Excited and yet nervous, filled with unimaginable longings.

This was only the second time they had spoken, and yet she felt drawn to him by an irresistible force. It was ridiculous! She could not possibly be falling in love with this man...or could she? No, no, of course she could not. She knew nothing about him. Yet what did she need to know other than the fact that he made her feel so alive?

Olivia schooled her unruly heart as the Captain's voice broke into her thoughts. 'What would you like me to fetch you?'

'Oh, just something light—a syllabub perhaps?'

Olivia sat down at the table Captain Denning had procured for them, watching as he threaded his way through the crowd milling around the sumptuous buffet tables. She thought he stood out from the other gentlemen, and not just because his hair was longer than most other men's. No, there was something about him—a presence: an air of mystery? Oh, she did not know! He was just different.

'Ah, there you are,' a soft voice said at her elbow. 'No, please do not get up, Miss Roade Burton. I came only to invite you to a little informal affair I am giving tomorrow evening at my brother's house. I have spoken to Lady Ravensden, and she is agreeable.'

'You are very kind, Lady Simmons.' Olivia smiled at her. 'If my sister has agreed, I shall be happy to come.'

'It is a very small affair. Nothing to compare with this, of course. But I like to gather a few friends at my table, and I have discovered that several of my close friends are visiting Brighton at the moment. I shall look forward to furthering my acquaintance with both you and Lady Ravensden.'

She nodded and moved off. Olivia glanced up and saw her speak to Captain Denning for a moment before he continued towards their table.

'I am told this is made with champagne and quite delicious,' Jack said, setting the delicate glass on the table in front of Olivia. He had also brought a flute of champagne for them both. 'You will forgive me if I do not eat? I dined earlier and I have no appetite.'

'You should perhaps eat more for your own good, sir,' Olivia said, then tasted her syllabub. 'Oh, this is delightful!'

'I am gratified,' Jack replied, a smile on his lips. 'Please do not scold me, Miss Roade Burton. Anne did so just now. I assure you, I am not so thin now as I was some weeks ago.'

Olivia's gaze went to the scar at his temple. 'Have you been recently wounded, Captain Denning?'

'At Badajoz,' he said, and his clipped tones warned her to ask no more questions.

Fortunately, Olivia was saved from any embarrassment at the sudden silence that fell between them by her sister's arrival.

Jack stood up as she approached. 'Lady Ravensden? You were pointed out to me earlier by mutual friends. May I be of service in fetching you some supper?'

'You are Captain Denning, of course,' Beatrice said, giving him a warm smile. 'Lady Simmons spoke of you—and I believe you rescued my sister from a rather fierce dog?'

'An unfortunate incident.' He inclined his head.

'But easily solved,' Beatrice said. 'In answer to your question, Captain Denning, I will have a syllabub if you will be so kind.'

Beatrice looked at Olivia as he went at once to fetch a glass of the creamy dessert for her.

'I do not think him odd, dearest. One can see he has been ill, of course, but he certainly has an air of distinction, and his manners cannot be faulted. He is clearly a gentleman, and a brave soldier. Lady Simmons told me he had been mentioned in despatches. I believe he may be due for an honour or a promotion of some kind.'

'A promotion? Do you suppose he means to return to his regiment once he has fully recovered?'

'Lady Simmons did not say. I imagine Captain Denning has done more than his share for his country already.'

Since the object of their very interesting discussion was making his way back to them, the conversation was turned. A ball was to be given at the Royal Pavilion quite soon, and would be even more prestigious than the one they had attended that evening.

'I do hope Harry will be here for the Regent's ball,' Beatrice said. 'I shall write and tell him so. Surely he cannot still be discussing Papa's project?'

'He will come if you write,' Olivia said. 'Shall we go home after supper?'

'If you wish,' Beatrice replied. 'But here is Captain Denning…'

They did not leave immediately after supper, however, for Captain Denning asked Olivia to stand up with him for the next set of country dances. After that, she was approached by two gentlemen she had known in London, both of whom were widowers some years older than Olivia, and both reputed to be looking for a wife.

It seemed that Captain Denning's interest in her had been noticed and had encouraged others to come forward. Her portion was not large, but ten thousand was not to be sneezed at, and, it seemed, some gentlemen might after all be prepared to take her despite the shadow of scandal attached to her name.

She danced with both gentlemen, but when she left the dance floor afterwards, it was to see Captain Denning on the verge of departing. He smiled and nodded to her, then went out alone. Lady Simmons had left some minutes earlier with her family. Beatrice asked if Olivia was ready to go, and she readily agreed. Somehow the bright aura of room seemed to have dimmed with Captain Denning's departure.

It was as they were being driven home in the carriage, that Beatrice spoke of what was on her mind.

'You must not be upset if everyone was not kind this evening, dearest,' she said. 'In time they will forget and accept you. I think you will find it will be easier when Harry comes.'

'Yes, I am sure of it,' Olivia said and smiled at her sister. 'Do not be anxious for me, Beatrice. I am not unhappy. It was a little uncomfortable at first this evening—but I managed to enjoy myself.'

'You seemed to enjoy waltzing with Captain Denning.' Beatrice gave her a teasing look.

'He dances expertly,' Olivia replied, then laughed. 'Oh, you know me too well! Captain Denning is obviously more accustomed to mixing in society than I imagined after our first meeting. And yes, I do like him, Beatrice. I like him very much.'

Beatrice nodded, her eyes sparkling with mischief. 'He is the grandson of the Earl of Heggan—a very old Irish title. His father is Viscount Stanhope, and I understand the English title was granted to the family for service to the Crown some sixty years back. I believe the Viscount is not a very nice man—but he and Captain Denning have nothing to say to one another. And his maternal grandfather, Sir Joshua Chambers, who was a much nicer man, recently bequeathed a very substantial fortune to the captain.'

'You have been busy!'

Beatrice laughed. 'Lady Simmons was most informative. I believe she is extremely fond of Captain Denning, just in a friendly way, you know. I found her a very pleasant companion.'

Olivia bit her lip. 'I have been given to understand their relationship is rather more intimate...'

'I believe it may have been before Captain Denning went out to the Peninsula,' Beatrice agreed. 'These things happen, Olivia, and should not be held against either party. Besides, Lady Simmons stressed that he had been kind to her when she was very unhappy, and that they have been family friends for years.'

Olivia digested this information in silence. Beatrice had clearly formed the opinion that the affair between Lady Simmons and Captain Denning was over.

Well, perhaps it was. Robina had only repeated what she had heard from someone else. She would not allow the rumour to cloud her judgement of either Lady Simmons or Captain Denning, she decided, as their carriage drew up outside the house.

Later, as Olivia was undressing, she pondered on

the reasons behind Lady Simmons's kindness to a girl she did not know. She had not only made it possible for Olivia to dance the waltz with Captain Denning, it seemed she had gone out of her way to make friends with Beatrice and pass on some very interesting information.

Why? Olivia might have suspected some devious purpose had she not instinctively taken to Lady Simmons. No, she must acquit her new acquaintance of having some unkind motive! So why had she pushed Olivia and Captain Denning together?

No obvious solution presented itself to Olivia, as she dismissed the maid Beatrice had sent to help her, ran a brush through her hair and climbed into her very comfortable goose-feather bed. Then she leaned over and blew out the candle on the cabinet beside her, a smile on her lips. It had been a pleasant evening after all.

For some reason she fell asleep almost at once. Her dreams were sweet, and featured strongly a certain gentleman, though in the morning she was unable to remember them at all.

Chapter Four

The next morning Beatrice again felt a little sleepy, but roused herself to go shopping with Olivia. They visited a fashionable milliner and purchased new bonnets, then bought gloves and a silk scarf for Olivia to take home as a gift for Nan.

Returning to the house for nuncheon, they found cards from several acquaintances of Beatrice's, and from two ladies who both had nephews known to be looking for a wife of some independent means.

'I can only think these cards were left for your benefit,' Beatrice said and laughed. 'Neither of the young gentlemen in question has a feather to fly with, I dare say. Your true situation must be beginning to filter through the grapevine, Olivia.'

'As if I would marry a fortune-hunter,' Olivia said with a frown. 'But I suppose ten thousand pounds does make me a little more acceptable.'

'Oh, depend upon it,' Beatrice quipped, smiling naughtily at her. 'There are several gentlemen I could mention who would be pleased to take you for a great deal less.'

Olivia laughed as she heard the teasing note in her sister's voice, then shook her head. 'You know I shall marry only if I fall in love the way you did, Beatrice.'

Beatrice smiled in a satisfied way but said nothing more. Olivia found herself blushing. She could not hide anything from her sister, but it would be foolish of her to make too much of Captain Denning's kindness the previous evening. He had neither said nor done anything to suggest that he had a *tendre* for her. As for Olivia's own feelings—that was another matter entirely.

Olivia knew that no other man of her acquaintance had ever made her feel the sensations which had flooded through her at his touch. Even as she struggled to deny it, her heart was telling her that she had at last found a man she could love.

No, no, it was quite ridiculous! She could not have fallen in love so suddenly. Why, Captain Denning was not even handsome—in the accepted way. Yet she had met many gentlemen who were perfect Adonises, and none of them had made the faintest impression on her unruly heart. Besides, she imagined that much of the Captain's gaunt look would disappear once his health improved.

Oh, what did it matter? Of course it could not. She had no reason to imagine that Captain Denning saw her as anything more than a pleasant dancing partner.

* * *

Beatrice and Olivia received three more callers that afternoon: Mr Reginald Smythe, Mr John Partridge, a rather worthy man with a substantial fortune of his own, and Lady Rowland, who had a young nephew of whom she was reputed to be fond. Each of them accepted an invitation to stay for tea, and Lady Rowland issued an invitation to a card party the following week.

'It is just a small affair,' she said. 'But I should be happy if you and your sister would care to attend, Lady Ravensden.'

'Yes, I believe we may manage it,' Beatrice replied, glancing towards the mantelpiece, where a growing number of invitations had been tucked into the elegant frame of the large mirror. 'Lord Ravensden should have joined us by then. He has been delayed by business.'

'Ah yes,' Lady Rowland nodded. 'I was sure that must be the case. There were rumours that it was otherwise—but people have such unfortunate tongues at times.'

'That explains your mixed reception last night,' Beatrice exclaimed after their visitors had supped their tea and departed. 'How vexing! People must have imagined Harry disapproved of my bringing you to Brighton. I shall write at once and…'

Whatever she had been about to say was lost as the front door bell pealed. Voices were heard in the hall, one of which caused Beatrice to rise joyfully to her feet. She looked towards the door in anticipation as her husband entered, still wearing clothes that were travel-stained.

'So there you are,' she cried. 'I was about to write to ask you to come with all speed...'

'Such impatience, my love,' Harry murmured, his eyes full of wicked mirth. 'Am I to conclude that I have been missed?'

'Harry, you wretch!' his wife said, giving him a reproving look. 'You must know you would always be missed—but it was for Olivia's sake that I meant to write.' She recounted her sister's unfortunate reception at the ball the previous evening. 'So you see, if it were not for Captain Denning, Olivia would have had an unhappy evening.'

Harry frowned. 'What fools people are! Forgive me, Olivia. I should have realised. I shall set things straight immediately.'

'I believe people are already beginning to change their minds,' Beatrice said. 'But we shall be more comfortable now you are here, dearest.'

He smiled at her. 'We shall give a dance of our own, Beatrice.'

'I had thought of a dinner...'

'Nothing so paltry,' he murmured. 'We may as well make a little stir, my love. Give the gossips something to talk about, why not?'

'Well, if you think so.' Beatrice looked pleased with the suggestion. 'We are dining with Lady Simmons and Captain Denning this evening. I am sure she would find you a place at her table...'

'We shall not trouble her this evening, Beatrice. You and Olivia must go, of course. I shall make my presence known in Brighton and do whatever needs to be done to scotch any undesirable rumours.'

It was but a short distance to the house at which Lady Simmons was staying under Lord Wilburton's protection. Harry, however, insisted on the two ladies being conveyed there in their carriage.

'A sedan chair is all very well,' he said, 'but I prefer you to have your own servants about you, my love. Especially when I cannot be with you.'

Beatrice did not object to his care of her as she might have once. She was feeling oddly lethargic and found that she enjoyed being fussed over a little.

'If you still feel tired in the mornings you should tell Harry,' Olivia said as they were being driven to their hostess's house that evening. 'It is not like you, Beatrice. You were always so full of energy.'

'I have become spoiled and lazy,' Beatrice replied, but her eyes did not quite meet those of her sister. 'Please do not say anything to Harry just yet.'

Olivia was thoughtful as she saw the faint blush in her cheeks. She suddenly realized what the cause of Beatrice's odd tiredness might be. However, she did not mention the possibility to her sister. If Beatrice were with child, she would naturally wish to tell her husband first.

Olivia felt a slight pang of envy. She had felt none when Beatrice married, rejoicing in the happiness of both her sister and Harry. Now, though, she was aware of feeling something she had not experienced before. How wonderful it would be to be married to a man she loved and anticipating the birth of his child!

Had she really imagined she would be happier living her life as a spinster? She saw now that it was only because she had thought herself unable to fall in love…as she undoubtedly had.

Every hour that passed was making it clearer to Olivia that she had somehow tumbled head over heels into a deep and passionate love. She had been waiting all day for the moment she would meet Captain Denning again. How foolish she was!

She must not betray herself! Olivia's cheeks felt warm as the groom helped first Beatrice and then her from the carriage. It would be humiliating if she were to show too plainly that she had given her heart to a man she hardly knew—and yet instinctively she did know him. He was the one man she could ever love.

She must not let him guess her feelings had gone so far. She must be friendly, welcoming to any advances he might make—but they must come from him. Olivia's pride would not allow her to set her cap at Captain Denning. No, she would keep a little distance between them, be a little restrained in her responses to him.

They were entering the house, being greeted by their hostess for the evening. Olivia smiled and curtsied slightly as she was introduced to Lord and Lady

Wilburton, then to Miss Rose, who was Lady Simmons's companion.

'How lovely to see you again,' Anne Simmons said. 'Do come into the withdrawing-room and meet more of my friends.'

Olivia went through the motions of meeting various ladies and gentlemen, but her gaze was drawn immediately to Captain Denning. He looked even more distinguished that evening in a coat of bottle green, which suited his colouring. How could she ever have mistaken him for a gamekeeper?

His expression softened a little as he saw her. He had been staring into the distance, as though not really a part of the company. Now he came towards her.

'Miss Roade Burton, good evening. It is pleasant to see you again. I was speaking to Anne earlier. She thought as it was your first visit to Brighton, you might like to see some of the places of interest—a drive to the Downs perhaps? Anne suggested a picnic and a visit to a particularly fine church she admires…'

'How kind of Lady Simmons to suggest it.' It was exactly the kind of outing Olivia would most enjoy, and would give her time to get to know her new friends a little better.

'We should go in a party, of course. If Lady Ravensden agrees.'

'I am sure she will,' Olivia said. 'Lord Ravensden arrived this afternoon. I believe he would wish to accompany us.'

'That would be perfect,' Jack replied. 'Lord

Ravensden may drive his wife if he so wishes, and I shall take you and Anne in my curricle.'

Olivia smiled. He was being so thoughtful, as was Lady Simmons. Why? Had they decided to take up the gauntlet against public opinion on her behalf? Or was there another, deeper reason?

'When shall we go?'

'Why not tomorrow noon if the weather is fine.' Lady Simmons said, coming up to them. 'I am glad my little jaunt found favour with you, Miss Roade Burton. It is a very pretty church, and the Downs are magnificent, of course.'

Olivia nodded. 'I could not ask for anything better,' she said. 'We must hope the weather stays warm and dry.'

'I am sure it will,' Lady Simmons said. 'My companion reads the seaweed, you know, and she believes we are due for a settled spell. Naturally, Dora will also be one of our party. You will not mind if she rides with you, Miss Roade Burton? I cannot deny poor Dora such a treat.'

'Of course I do not mind,' Olivia replied. She hesitated, then, 'I should be happy if you would call me, Olivia, ma'am. At least in private. We do not need to be too formal, I hope?'

'Of course not, my dear.'

Olivia blushed as she felt Captain Denning's eyes upon her.

'Tell me, Miss Olivia,' he said. 'Do you play

bridge or whist? Anne is a clever bridge partner, but my preference is for whist.'

'Captain Denning is an exacting partner,' their hostess warned. 'He does not suffer fools gladly, Olivia. You should be wary of him.'

'Anne, you are unfair,' he protested but with a smile on his lips. 'I like to win,' he explained to Olivia. 'Though I seldom gamble for high stakes. It is not the prize but the game that matters—do you not agree?'

'Oh, yes,' she said, unconsciously meeting the challenge in his eyes with one of her own. 'The pleasure of pitting one's wits against others. Not for gain but for it's own sake.'

'I see we think alike,' Jack Denning remarked. 'I believe we should not be partners, Miss Olivia. It would be more interesting to contest the issue…Anne shall be my partner this evening, and you shall play with a fourth person.'

Olivia lowered her gaze. Was she wrong to imagine that he was flirting with her a little? Or was he merely teasing her? She saw that he had cast off the dark mood which had held him in thrall at their first meeting. Why was that? Because of her—or for some other reason?

Olivia quickly smothered the green-eyed imp of jealousy that invaded her thoughts. She had no right to be jealous even if Lady Simmons was his mistress. None at all! They had both offered her friendship at a time when she had sorely needed it, and she was grateful.

If her foolish heart had surrendered too easily, that was her own fault. She would not allow the seed of jealousy to rob her of her peace of mind, nor would she betray her innermost feelings.

'I shall look forward to the contest, sir,' she said with a lift of her chin. 'But be warned. I do not give way easily.'

'No,' Jack replied. 'I did not imagine you would, Miss Olivia.'

The remainder of the evening passed very pleasantly. Indeed, Olivia could not recall ever having enjoyed herself in company so well. She genuinely liked and admired Lady Simmons, who that evening was looking rather lovely in her gown of silver tissue. However, the spice was provided for Olivia by Captain Denning's enigmatic glances, and the challenge of pitting her wits against a demon card player, for he was certainly that.

She herself partnered Lord Wilburton, a kindly, cheerful man, who was no novice at the game. In the end the honours were even, for though Olivia and her partner managed to win the first three hands, they afterwards went down hand after hand. However, since they were playing for minimal stakes, there was no great loss to anyone.

'I vow we did not deserve to lose, Miss Olivia,' Lord Wilburton declared when the cards were abandoned in favour of a light supper. 'You played well, m'dear. I believe I threw away that last hand.'

Olivia assured him it was no such thing. 'I believe Captain Denning was just too good for us,' she said and laughed.

She was still smiling as she and Beatrice took their leave later.

'We shall see you both tomorrow,' Jack Denning said. 'I hope you are not too cross with me for winning, Miss Olivia?'

'I shall come about,' she told him, her eyes bright with excitement. 'I do not intend to give you best, sir. One day I shall win.'

'Perhaps.' He looked amused. 'I shall look forward to many future contests, Miss Olivia.'

She gave him an arch look but would not be drawn further.

Beatrice glanced at her when they were being driven home. 'You enjoyed yourself this evening, I think?'

'Yes, very much. I have seldom found company more pleasing.'

Since their hostess, her family and friends were all some years older than Olivia, it was clear to her sister that Olivia's pleasure in the evening could have only one source.

'Captain Denning seems to be a charming man,' she said. 'A little stern in his looks on occasion, but thoughtful. It would be wonderful if…but I rush on too fast. You have only just become acquainted. We must not hope for too much too soon, dearest.'

Olivia blushed. Beatrice was very gently warning her not to place her hopes too high. She knew that her sister was merely trying to protect her, but she could not hide her feelings from Beatrice.

'I know it is foolish of me,' she confessed. 'But I believe my affections are already engaged. I hope I did not show my preference too plainly this evening?'

'No, I am sure not,' Beatrice replied, smiling at her reassuringly. 'I may have guessed something had changed in you, but no one else would notice anything untoward. Although you responded to Captain Denning's challenge, you showed nothing more than high spirits. Indeed, you seemed as much at ease with Lord Wilburton.'

'He was kind to me, and not in the least ill-tempered because we lost,' Olivia said. 'I liked him very well—as I did his wife.'

'I am sure no one could fault your behaviour at all, dearest.'

Olivia was reassured by Beatrice's remarks. She went to bed feeling happy and looking forward to their outing the next day.

Fortunately, the weather held and the sun was warm as they set out. Harry was driving Beatrice and Lady Simmons, and Captain Denning took up Olivia and Miss Rose.

'This little trip was such a delightful thought,' Miss

Rose remarked to Olivia as they set out just behind the first vehicle. 'But dear Lady Simmons is always so kind and generous.'

'Yes, I have found her so,' Olivia agreed.

The companion frowned. 'It is such an unfortunate thing…her husband, you know. He has been unkind to her. Most unkind…'

Since Miss Rose was a gentle, placid creature, who usually kept her own counsel, this statement, and the force with which it was spoken, could not but make an impression on Olivia. She did not enquire further, however, for Lady Simmons's marital problems were not her affair.

There was little chance for conversation with Captain Denning as he negotiated the town and then set out at a good pace along the highway. It was only when they reached a pleasant spot high on the South Downs that they had a chance to speak to one another properly.

'Am I forgiven this morning?' he asked, as he handed the reins to a groom and jumped down to help the ladies. He smiled as he gave his hand to Olivia. 'I believe I was a little unkind last evening.'

'Not at all, sir,' Olivia said. 'I am not such a poor mouse as to repine over a little setback.'

'No, I do not believe anyone could describe you in such a way,' he replied.

The look in his eyes at that moment made her blush and avert her gaze. He seemed to be considering her, as though analysing her character. Olivia wondered what could lie behind such a look. Was it possible that he was as interested in her as she in him?

Olivia, Beatrice and Lady Simmons took a little stroll in the sunshine. High on the Downs, the view was magnificent, a cloudless blue sky and in the distance a sparkling, restless sea.

Miss Rose had insisted that she would stay behind to help the servants set up their picnic. Cushions were placed on the dry grass for the ladies, and the gentlemen lounged on rugs spread at their feet. Butlers' trays were rested on little stands and large hampers opened to display a sumptuous buffet.

The conversation was general. Harry and Captain Denning seemed to take to one another at once, as had Beatrice and Anne Simmons. They all laughed a great deal and, warmed by a gentle sun, Olivia was aware of a feeling of content.

She tried not to put herself forward, but responded to Captain Denning's remarks in a friendly, easy manner, taking care not to let her feelings show too plainly. She had taken Beatrice's gentle warning to heart. It would not do to expect too much, and yet she believed her feelings must be returned. Surely it was not possible for her to feel so deeply if he was indifferent?

'So, Miss Olivia,' he asked when there was a sudden lull in the conversation. 'What do you think of the Pavilion?'

'It is most unusual,' she ventured.

The Regent's house had once been a pleasant but

ordinary residence, but he was gradually transforming it into an exotic palace with domes and spires, which were rather outrageous if the truth were told.

'Unusual? Yes, it is certainly that,' Jack agreed. 'Your restraint does you credit, Miss Olivia.'

Olivia only smiled and refused to be drawn. Conversation became general once more, and then, their picnic over, the party drove on to the village of Piddinghoe.

The flint cottages and twisting main street were picturesque, but it was the church that Lady Simmons had brought them to see.

'It has one of the only three Norman round towers in Sussex,' she told Olivia as they walked together in the churchyard. The grass had just been mown and the sharp smell of it mingled with wild roses in the hedgerows was the scent of summer. 'Do you not think it very lovely?'

'Yes, it is beautiful,' Olivia agreed. 'Thank you for suggesting the visit. I have so much enjoyed myself.'

They were strolling now by the banks of the river Ouse, along which the village bordered. Lady Simmons glanced at her, a slightly puzzled expression in her eyes.

'Have you, my dear? I thought you seemed a little subdued earlier.'

'Oh, I was just feeling lazy because the sun was so warm.'

Lady Simmons nodded, accepting her answer. 'It

is very warm today,' she said, 'though one always feels a little breeze on the Downs.'

Olivia smiled but saw no need to elaborate. Harry and Captain Denning were waiting by their separate carriages. They appeared to be having a serious conversation, but broke it off as the ladies arrived.

'Ah, there you all are,' Harry said. 'Denning was about to come in search of you. We thought you must have been locked in the crypt.'

'We did not see the crypt, even if there was one,' Beatrice said with a shake of her head. 'But I am glad Captain Denning was concerned enough to rescue us, had we needed it.'

Harry gave her a wicked look, which she ignored.

Jack Denning came forward to help Miss Rose and then Olivia into his curricle. Olivia thought his expression serious, the haunted look she had believed banished lurking in his eyes. What could have brought it back? Perhaps the rather serious conversation he had been having with Harry?

'Did you enjoy your visit to the church?'

'Very much. It has more style than the Pavilion, I think.'

'I see you have taste as well as beauty.' He smiled at her, his expression becoming less stern. 'I think we must begin to make our way home. I have an engagement for this evening.'

Olivia nodded. 'You were generous to give up so much of your time for us, sir.'

'It was a pleasure. Perhaps you will allow me to take you for a drive along the seafront one morning?'

'I should be glad to go with you, Captain Denning.'

He nodded, a thoughtful look on his face. 'In eight days' time we shall all be attending the Regent's ball. I trust you do mean to be there, Miss Olivia?'

'Yes, indeed,' she said, her head lifting a little. 'I am looking forward to it very much...'

Over the next few days, Olivia seemed to meet Captain Denning almost everywhere. He called to take her driving most mornings, and they met in the evening on five separate occasions, including Lady Rossiter's soirée, though on that occasion Captain Denning soon disappeared into the card room with most of the other gentlemen. But on the evening prior to the Regent's ball, they were all invited to Lady Carne's house for dinner.

'You must promise to waltz with me at least once, Miss Olivia,' Jack declared as they spoke of the ball. 'Or I shall think myself slighted.'

Olivia smiled. Although several card tables had been set up that evening, they had not had the opportunity of playing against one another, but their verbal banter continued the challenge that had begun at Lady Simmons's house.

'Perhaps if I am very favoured, you might save two for me?'

'I might,' Olivia teased. 'The first waltz and the supper dance perhaps?'

'I shall take that as a solemn promise.'

Olivia could hardly be blamed if she believed his teasing, enigmatic glances meant that his interest was engaged. She tried to keep her head, but it was difficult when she found herself engulfed by a tide of emotions she had never experienced before. So, meeting Robina Perceval out walking on the morning of the Regent's ball, she was surprised at her friend's odd manner when Captain Denning's name came into their conversation.

'What are you thinking?' Olivia asked, wrinkling her brow. 'I know there is something on your mind.'

Robina blushed, looking awkward. 'I know you like him, Olivia—but I think you should be careful of him,' she said. 'People say…odd things of him.'

'I don't understand. What kind of things?'

'I heard that he had quarrelled with both his father and grandfather…' Robina hesitated, then: 'They say he has refused to visit his father, who is dying—and he has sworn never to marry. He dislikes and distrusts women.'

'Oh, surely not!' cried Olivia, whose experience of the Captain had been very different. 'He is always so pleasant and charming to me and to every lady he meets.'

'I know he seems to be,' Robina agreed. 'But Lady Exmouth heard that he has refused to do his duty by the Heggan family. Lord Heggan told him he must marry and provide the family with an heir—and he refused.'

'Oh, is that all?' Olivia laughed at her friend's serious expression. 'Perhaps he simply does not wish to marry for such a reason.'

Her unruly heart took Captain Denning's refusal to do his duty by the family as a sign that, like her, the Captain would marry only for love. It confirmed all her romantic ideals, and made her even more sure that he was the man she could love.

She was eager for their meeting that night and unheeding of her friend's warning, because she knew it was already too late for caution. She had fallen deeply in love for the first time in her life, and was determined that she would have Jack Denning for her husband or no one.

Chapter Five

'You might perhaps have a word with Olivia, dearest,' Harry Ravensden remarked to his wife as he dismissed her maid after she had finished dressing that evening. 'Here, let me fasten that necklace.' His fingers lightly caressed the back of her neck. 'Beautiful…quite lovely.' It was his wife he was referring to, not the new pendant necklace of emeralds and diamonds he had just given her.

'You spoil me, Harry.' Beatrice turned to gaze up at him, her eyes lovelier to him than any jewels. 'I know what you mean, of course. Olivia is obviously in love, though she tries to hide it behind a flirtatious manner.'

'Nevertheless, her preference for Denning has been remarked,' Harry said with a frown. 'I simply feel she ought to be careful. You know how people love to talk. After the unfortunate episode last year…she needs to be even more circumspect than other young ladies are. Otherwise, her reputation could be damaged further.'

'Oh, surely not?' Beatrice was immediately concerned for her sister. 'She has done nothing wrong, Harry.'

'No, of course not. I did not mean to imply that she had. Certainly not! It was always more my fault than Olivia's. I meant only to point out that this could rebound on Olivia if Denning does not come up to scratch.'

'Do you think he will not?' Beatrice looked at him anxiously.

'I have heard that he has refused to marry to oblige Lord Heggan. From my own observations, I would say Denning is attracted to Olivia, but not contemplating marriage at this moment.'

'Oh, Harry,' Beatrice cried. 'I do pray you are wrong. I should hate Olivia to be hurt…'

'So would I,' Harry agreed. He as much as his wife understood that they both owed a great deal to Olivia. 'Would you like me to have a discreet word with Denning—warn him that he should back off now if he has no serious intentions towards her?'

'Would he not resent that, Harry?'

'I would willingly incur Denning's displeasure to protect your sister, dearest. Far better that he should feel himself insulted than that she should be misled into giving her heart unwisely.'

Beatrice nodded but made no reply. She was very much afraid that Olivia's heart had already been given to Captain Denning. Yet Harry would know how to put the matter delicately, and it might be that they were worrying for no good reason.

'Yes, perhaps you should have a word with him, Harry,' she said. 'Explain that she has been hurt and that her family wants only to protect her from more gossip...'

Happily unaware that her sister and Harry Ravensden were so earnestly discussing her, Olivia finished preparing for the ball. She was wearing a very pretty lemon silk ball gown. The neckline dipped into a V at both the back and front, but the back had gathered frills right to the tip of the little train, which looked very stylish and elegant, and there were knots of silk flowers at her breasts. Her long gloves were white, as were her slippers, and her hair was caught into ringlets with a white ribbon.

She wore only a fine gold chain with the cross Mrs Roade had given her about her neck, for she had very little jewellery. Just some trinkets Beatrice had given her and some simple beads. All her costly jewels had been left behind when she left the home of her adoptive parents.

It was odd, Olivia thought, but Lady Burton had been much in her mind that day. She had tried these past months not to think of the woman who had been as a mother to her for so many years, but sometimes the memories came back to haunt her.

Lord Burton had always been stern, though he had

undoubtedly spoiled Olivia in a material way. Yet she had never been truly convinced of his true affection for her. She rather thought he had seen her as a pretty ornament, a bauble his wealth had bought for him. Sometimes, as she grew older, she had not quite liked the way he looked at her…almost as though he saw her as something other than the indulged daughter he claimed her to be.

Olivia had had no such doubts concerning Lady Burton's feelings. She was sure her adoptive mother had loved her. After the breach between them, she had been terribly hurt that her adoptive mother had allowed her to be cast out, but the months spent in contemplation since then had led her to realize that her mama had really been given no choice.

Perhaps Beatrice was right. Perhaps some attempt at reconciliation with Lady Burton should be made.

'Are you ready, dearest?' Olivia's thoughts were interrupted as her sister entered the bedchamber. 'Oh, you do look lovely this evening!'

'Thank you,' Olivia said and smiled at her. 'You look wonderful, Beatrice—there is a glow about you.'

'I feel wonderful.' Beatrice touched the emerald necklace at her throat, her cheeks a little pink. 'Harry gave me these this evening. He had meant them for my birthday, but he was excited by my news…'

Olivia nodded, then moved to kiss her cheek. 'I believe you are to be congratulated, Beatrice.'

'So you guessed.' Beatrice laughed. 'I did not want to say until I was certain. I told Harry earlier that I suspected I might be increasing, and he admitted that he had had his own suspicions. Harry will summon a doctor soon, but I feel fairly certain I am with child.'

'I am so glad. You must both be very happy?'

'Yes. We are, of course…' Beatrice hesitated, but could not bring herself to speak to Olivia about Captain Denning. After all, perhaps Harry was wrong in his opinion that the Captain had no thought of marriage. 'I should like to see you as happy, Olivia.'

'I am much happier than I was,' Olivia replied, smiling at her. 'Oh, I know I should not allow myself to hope—but I cannot help it. I do know that I shall never marry, unless…' She paused and blushed. 'But I have no need to explain to you. You fell in love with Harry at first sight.'

Beatrice smiled and hid her anxiety. She did understand exactly how Olivia felt. She had gone through a period of uncertainty and distress until Harry had been free to offer her his love.

'Shall we go?' she said, holding her hand out to Olivia. 'We do not want to miss anything. I am sure it will be a sad crush, but I mean to dance this evening—if Harry can be kept from the card tables for long enough to oblige me.'

It was a glittering occasion. The Pavilion was remarkable enough from the outside, but the interior had been furnished in the Chinese taste, which looked very odd in Olivia's opinion, though many professed to admire it. The rooms were also overpoweringly hot, and the ladies were all using their fans to good effect.

Everyone was wearing his or her finest clothes and most costly jewels, which flashed in the lights of the brilliant chandeliers. As Beatrice had forecast, it was indeed a sad crush, the rooms overflowing with laughing, chattering people, who all seemed to know one another. However, as Olivia found herself besieged by eager partners as soon as she entered the ballroom, she hardly had time to notice the overcrowding.

Harry had done his work well. Olivia was once again recognized as an heiress, and several impecunious young men felt the risk of being jilted by her was worth taking. For who knew, she might not change her mind a second time, and she was certainly a prize to be gained. And when the Regent himself went so far as to smile and speak to her kindly for several minutes soon after her arrival, her success was assured.

Olivia's card was quickly filled, but she had pencilled Captain Denning's name in two spaces, and as soon as the first waltz was announced, he came to her side.

'My dance, I believe, Miss Olivia?'

Her heart leapt. 'Let me see…' She pretended to consult her card. 'Why yes, sir, I believe you are right.'

Jack's eyes gleamed. He took her arm firmly and led her out to join the other dancers.

'I believe you are a minx, Miss Olivia.'

'How can you say so, Captain Denning?' She gave him a wicked glance, her eyes bright with mischief.

'With perfect truth,' he replied and, placing his hand at her waist, swept her away into the crowd of swirling dancers.

At their first meeting Olivia had been afraid of his dog, appearing to be a little timid; at their second she must have seemed to be a rather sad creature, forced to sit out most of the dances for lack of a partner. This evening she was once again the popular Miss Roade Burton, who had taken the Ton by storm.

Olivia sensed that Captain Denning was a little surprised at the transformation. She felt there was an odd reserve in his manner that evening—almost a withdrawal. Did he think her a flirt? Gazing up at him anxiously, she saw that his eyes seemed to be looking beyond her.

Had she done something to make him angry? Olivia could not imagine what that might be—unless he was jealous?

Her heart beat a little faster as the thought entered her mind. Oh, if only it were so! If only he would speak!

'Shall you be at Lady Ravensden's dance next week, sir?'

'I fear not,' Jack replied, glancing down at her. 'I am recalled home on business. I leave on Sunday.'

Only two days away! Olivia's heart sank. So little time left to her—and then she might never see him again.

'We shall miss you,' she said, speaking honestly. 'I believe my sister intends a stay of at least another week.'

'Oh, you will not miss one acquaintance amongst so many,' Jack said, ignoring the appeal in her lovely eyes. 'I am sure you will have forgotten me within the week.'

'I am sure I shall not, sir.'

Their dance was ending. Olivia noticed Captain Denning's quick frown as he prepared to lead her back to her sister. She sensed that something was on his mind. His manner had most definitely changed towards her, was not so outgoing as before. Why? What had caused him to withdraw his friendship?

She wanted to ask him, but knew she dared not. Instead, she flashed a brilliant smile at him, a teasing sparkle in her eyes.

'You will not forget we are engaged for the supper dance?'

'No, I shall not forget.' He smiled, bowed and walked away into the throng.

Olivia's eyes followed him, her wistful expression betraying more of her thoughts and feelings than she realized before she turned to greet her next partner.

From across the room, Lady Clements observed the revealing look and frowned as she spoke to her nephew. 'You should make a push to engage the interest of Miss Roade Burton,' she told him sharply. 'Else you will lose your chance to secure her fortune.

Ten thousand is not as much as she might have had perhaps, but it is a useful sum.'

'B-but what can I do?' asked Mr Reginald Smythe. 'She hardly notices me. And it is not just because of Denning. She has so many admirers since it became common knowledge that she is not penniless after all.'

'Do not be so weak-willed,' Lady Clements said, giving him a sour look. 'You have debts of nearly five thousand, and neither your mama nor I are prepared to pay them for you. Unless you do something you will find yourself in a debtor's prison.'

Reginald Smythe nodded gloomily. He had been a fool to gamble for stakes he could not afford, and he knew it was hopeless to apply to any member of his family for help. Unless he could think of a way to attract the interest of an heiress, he would very likely be ruined. Yet what could he do?

'Miss Roade Burton is in an awkward position. Her reputation is fragile after that last contretemps,' Lady Clements remarked acidly. 'It should not be beyond your imagination to compromise the girl in some way. Take her out into the garden or to one of the private rooms. I will engage to follow with her sister—or better still, Lord Ravensden. If we catch you behaving badly, I will insist you do the honourable thing and marry the chit!'

Reginald looked at her in amazement. It was a daring plan, but not at all what he might have expected to hear from his respectable aunt.

'I'll take her to one of the private rooms just off the ballroom,' he said, a thoughtful expression in his eyes. 'Far more intimate than the garden, don't you think?'

Unaware that Lady Clements and her nephew were hatching schemes to entrap her into marriage, Olivia continued to dance the night away. Although she looked for him often, she saw no sign of Captain Denning in the ballroom. She supposed that he must have gone to the card room, preferring like some other gentlemen to spend his time gaming.

In thinking that, however, she wronged him. Jack had gone into the garden to smoke a cigar and think. His conversation with Harry Ravensden earlier that evening had given him food for thought—thoughts which were not affording him a great deal of pleasure at that moment.

He had carelessly taken up the cudgels on Miss Roade Burton's behalf after seeing her humiliation at Lady Clements's ball because he hated the hypocrisy in society, and because something in him had responded to her brave attempt to ignore what was happening to her. Once they began to talk and to know one another, he had found himself caught by her naughty looks and smiles.

Jack sensed there was far more to Olivia than he might have imagined from her society manners, and perhaps it was this that had led him into what he saw as a mild flirtation. He had not thought beyond the next few days…until this evening. If the world of polite society and Miss Roade Burton were expecting a proposal, they would be sadly disappointed.

Yes, she was charming. Yes, she amused him with her challenging looks—and yes, he was physically attracted to her, felt protective of her in a way he had not felt before, but that did not mean he was thinking of making her his wife. Jack had his own reasons for refraining from matrimony, and he had never revealed the whole of them to anyone. Not even to Anne, who had once been his lover, and was now his friend, had he ever confessed his worst nightmare.

No, he would be a fool to think of Olivia! It was an impossible situation. If Jack had ever contemplated more than a flirtation between them, he had been warned to think again. Ravensden had made it abundantly clear that he would protect Olivia's reputation no matter what.

The intervention had angered Jack. Good grief! Did Ravensden imagine he planned the girl's ruin? He of all men! To harm a woman in any way was something Jack would never wish to do, something so foreign to his nature that had he not perfectly understood Ravensden's point of view, he might have challenged him to a duel for the insult.

So, if he did not plan Olivia's seduction or marriage, what were his intentions?

Jack scowled at his own thoughts. He disliked his affairs being scrutinised so intimately. Damn Ravensden! What business was it of his? Yet he could not fault the other man's thinking. It was true that

Jack had paid Olivia particular attention. If he continued to do so, it would undoubtedly lead to speculation, which in turn might damage Olivia in some way: her reputation, if not her heart. For he was uncertain of her feelings towards him. Sometimes her smile seemed to hint at more than mere friendship, but he had seen her smile at others as warmly.

His only choice was to draw back now. He had no right to marry a girl like that! She was too lovely, too far above him—too innocent to guess at the blackness he kept hidden in his heart.

Making up his mind, he flicked away his cigar into the bushes. The honourable thing would be to act immediately. He would find Olivia, apologise and leave without taking her to supper.

At the same moment that Jack was coming to his decision, Olivia was looking ruefully at the hem of her gown. It had just been trodden on and torn by the clumsy Mr Reginald Smythe, who had come to claim his dance.

'Your pretty gown is ruined,' he said and blushed as he apologised for the fourth time in quick succession. 'What can I do to make amends? I am so very sorry.'

'Do not worry,' Olivia replied, smothering her sigh of annoyance. He looked so wretched that she felt sorry for him. 'I shall find somewhere to be private and pin up the tear.'

'Do you carry something in your reticule?' he asked, looking eager. 'May I be of assistance? I could show you a room nearby—and perhaps I could help you to make the repair?'

Had he been one of the hardened rakes, some of whom had pursued her relentlessly when she was in London, Olivia might have been more wary. However, Reginald Smythe was such a diffident, unsure young man that she believed herself safe in trusting him, and smiled her agreement.

'Pray let us go at once,' she said. 'I certainly cannot dance until the hem has been repaired.'

She left the ballroom and went into the small parlour just along the hallway, followed meekly by Mr Smythe. Closing the door behind them, he went across to a small sofa and set a branch of candles on a wine table next to it so that she might see more clearly.

'If you were to sit down,' he suggested, 'I could lift the hem so that you could pin it into place.'

Olivia frowned. She had suddenly realized that her being here alone with him, in what was an intimate situation, might look odd if someone were to come in. She ought of course to have gone upstairs to the room provided for the ladies, where an attendant might have pinned the torn hem for her. Yet surely it could not matter? It would take only a moment to make the repair, and then they could return to the ballroom.

She sat down, and Mr Smythe knelt at her feet, handing her the torn hem carefully so that she could do what was needed. She set several tiny stitches, and replaced the sewing packet in her beaded purse.

'There, that was soon done,' she said, feeling relieved. 'Thank you, sir. I believe we should go back now.'

'No! Not yet,' he cried. Olivia was startled by the look of desperation in his face. He threw a scared glance over his shoulder, then grabbed hold of her hand. 'I brought you here in order to be alone with you, Miss Olivia. Pray forgive me, but you must know that I have fallen in love with you. I am desperate. If you will not marry me, I do not know what I shall do…'

'Pray do not…' He was still kneeling at her feet. Olivia was shocked by the wildness in his eyes, and knew she had been unwise to come here with him. 'I am honoured by your offer, of course, but I must refuse. I cannot return your kind regard, sir. I must ask you to release my hand and…'

He threw another terrified glance towards the door, then flung his body forward, forcing her back on the sofa, his whole weight pressing on her. Olivia found herself crushed beneath him, unable to move as his hands pawed at her breasts, and his mouth covered hers in a wet kiss that sent a shiver of revulsion through her. She pushed at his shoulders, moving her head in a violent protest.

'No! No, please do not…let me go at once!'

'I suggest you do as Miss Roade Burton asks!'

The cold angry voice startled her eager seducer,

and he jerked back, his eyes popping in dismay as he stared at Captain Denning, who was standing in the doorway.

'W-what are you doing here?' he mumbled stupidly. 'It was supposed to be my aunt and...' He stopped, looking terrified as he saw the dark eyes narrow dangerously. 'I—I mean...'

'I am well aware of your meaning, and your actions,' Jack said, mouth hard, expression thunderous. 'You are a knave and a fool, sir. How dare you behave in such a despicable way? I suggest you get out now. Before I forget that you are merely a clumsy youth and decide to teach you some manners.'

'Yes...of course... F-forgive me.'

Reginald Smythe was suddenly up and running like a startled hare.

Released, Olivia sat up very straight. Her cheeks were burning and she felt mortified and extremely foolish.

'I have been careless,' she faltered. 'I never expected him to...'

'You have been subjected to the wiles of a very foolish young man and his scheming aunt,' Jack said, walking towards her as she rose uncertainly to her feet. 'Nothing can excuse their behaviour, but you have only to take this lesson to heart. Men are not to be trusted, Olivia. Even the best of them can act like beasts at times.'

Olivia was shocked by his haunted expression. What had caused him to look like that? Surely not just the clumsy attempt at seduction he had prevented by his timely arrival?

'He seemed so harmless, but I should have been more careful.' She blushed. 'I did not think...'

Jack frowned as he saw that the silk roses at her breast had been torn away from her gown in the struggle.

'Damn the young fool,' he muttered, furious suddenly. 'I should have thrashed him. He deserves no less!'

'It does not matter. You were in time to—to...' She blushed again and could not continue.

'Your gown is torn. Do you have a pin?'

'Yes, I think so.' Olivia glanced down at herself. 'It is awkward. I am not sure I can manage it...'

'Allow me.' Jack took the pin, then, seeing the obvious distress she was still suffering, he reached out to touch her cheek. 'Forgive me for not coming sooner. I saw you enter this room with Mr Smythe when I came in from the garden, but I hesitated to follow, thinking that...'

'Surely not that I wanted to be alone with him?' Olivia gazed up into his troubled eyes. 'He trod on the hem of my gown and tore it, then offered to help me...a plot to be alone with me, I see it now, but then I thought him too shy. I was wrong, but you cannot believe I provoked that scene just now? That I wanted him to make love to me?'

'No, of course not.' Jack seemed unsure. 'Yet some men will take a flirtatious glance to mean more than a lady may intend. Especially young whelps with no manners!'

'I did not flirt with him. You must believe me,' Olivia said earnestly. 'I do not care for anyone but…' She stopped and blushed furiously as she realized what she had almost said.

Jack frowned. His eyes looked deep into hers as though searching for something, then, without conscious thought of what he did, he bent his head to kiss her lips. At first it was a sweet, gentle caress, but Olivia's instant response drew a fierce reaction from him. His arms went around her and he drew her to him, holding her close but with such a gentle care that she felt her head swooning from the delicious sensations he was arousing in her. Now his kiss deepened hungrily, his tongue plundering the fresh sweetness of her mouth, his lips demanding and yet giving so sweetly that she felt no fear of his embrace, only an answering need within herself.

Neither of them was aware of the door opening behind them until a woman's startled cry made them break away guiltily. As they both looked towards the doorway, it was to see Lady Clements's surprise turn to annoyance. Just behind her stood Lord Ravensden, a severe frown making him look unusually stern. Olivia was very conscious of the torn roses at her breast, and of how the condition of her gown must appear—as if it had been ripped in a passionate embrace between them! What must Lady Clements and Lord Ravensden be thinking of her?

For a moment there was cold anger in Harry's eyes, then he was suddenly smiling, but it was not his usual friendly smile that he directed at Jack. His eyes had the quality of ice, his manner distinctly threatening as he said, 'I take it I am to wish you happy, Denning?' His words had the thrust of cold steel, leaving the other gentleman in no doubt of his meaning. If the answer were not to his liking, there might be blood spilled that night.

Jack's hesitation was momentary before he inclined his head. He did not fear to meet Ravensden in a duel, but would be loath to take life needlessly. Besides, the answer was suddenly so simple.

'I am in that fortunate position, Lord Ravensden. As you know, we spoke earlier of the matter. I am happy to inform you that Olivia has done me the honour of accepting my offer of marriage.'

Harry nodded, his expression altering not one whit as he glanced at Olivia's shocked face. 'I congratulate you, Denning. You have made a wise choice. Olivia my dear, I should like to wish you happy.'

'Perhaps you would care to announce our engagement this evening?' Jack asked. 'Olivia had a little accident with her gown. We shall return to the ballroom together once she has had time to make the repair.'

'Well, really!' Lady Clements exclaimed. She was quite unable to hide her annoyance at finding Captain Denning apparently seducing Olivia instead of her nephew, and the news of their engagement brought a sour expression to her thin face. 'I thought…but it seems I was wrong. Pray excuse me.' She walked away, her back stiff.

Harry frowned as she closed the door behind her sharply. 'Lady Clements insisted I accompany her here. She insinuated that Olivia was in trouble, and I felt obliged to come. I imagine I was supposed to force you into marriage with her nephew, Olivia,' he said. 'I apologise for allowing my better judgement to be swayed, but I hoped to contain the damage. However, once she had seen you together in that way, I fear there was no help for it. It is a damned coil!'

'You mistake the matter,' Jack said, and his tone was icy with pride. 'Your arrival made no difference, Ravensden. Olivia had that moment accepted my offer and it was only a matter of time before we came in search of you and Lady Ravensden.'

'Is that so, Olivia?' Harry asked. 'Do you truly consent of your own free will to this marriage?'

She lifted her head proudly. 'Captain Denning rescued me from an attempt by Lady Clements's nephew to seduce me. I struggled and my gown was torn. Mr Smythe's behaviour distressed me, and Captain Denning comforted me. We found ourselves overwhelmed by our feelings for one another.'

Harry's expression lightened. 'In that case I must offer you both my sincere good wishes for your future happiness. I am delighted for you both, and I apologise for misjudging you, Denning. If you will excuse me, I shall find Beatrice and tell her the good news.

I know she will be pleased that it is settled between you.'

A short silence fell between Olivia and Jack as he went out, leaving them together. Then Olivia gazed up at Jack, her eyes bright with the tears she refused to shed.

'You do not have to marry me,' she said bravely. 'We could wait for a while and then break off our engagement…'

'Is that what you would prefer, Olivia?'

She continued to gaze into his eyes for a moment, then shook her head. 'No, it is not—but you were obliged to speak as you did. I am offering you the chance to withdraw, if not now then at a later time.'

Jack reached for her hand. He carried it to his lips, turning it to place a kiss within the soft palm.

'I do not wish to withdraw,' he said softly. 'I am not worthy of you, but I should be honoured if you would in truth consent to be my wife, Miss Olivia.'

'I am both grateful for and honoured by your offer, sir,' Olivia replied, making him a little curtsey. 'I would be very happy to become your wife.'

'Then the matter is settled,' Jack said. 'Would you wish to be married in town—or from your home?'

'I—I have not thought.' Olivia was suddenly a little shy of him. It had all happened so swiftly that she had hardly had time to catch her breath. 'Perhaps we should discuss the details with my sister?'

'Yes, of course. I shall call tomorrow morning at noon. I am sure Lady Ravensden will know what is best,' Jack agreed. 'And now—if you will allow me? I should pin your gown.'

Olivia nodded. She stood without moving, hardly daring to breathe as he pinned the roses into place, his fingers just brushing against the delicate hollow between her breasts. Her heart was racing wildly. She wondered if he guessed how much the intimate act had affected her, but as she glanced up into his eyes, his expression sent a chill down her spine. He seemed so serious!

'Captain Denning...'

'Jack,' he corrected and smiled at her. 'Do not be nervous, Olivia. I shall never hurt you or abuse you. I promise you that faithfully. Indeed, I shall do my best to make you happy, my dear.'

Olivia nodded. Her gown was now perfectly respectable. She took his arm and they went out together, back to the ballroom to join their friends.

'If you will permit me, I should like to give you a special wedding,' Beatrice said to her sister later. They were alone in Olivia's bedroom, and it was past two o'clock in the morning. 'We could hold it at Camberwell, and Papa and Nan can stay with us. The house is large enough for you to invite as many of your friends as you wish, dearest.'

'You are so good to me!' Olivia moved to embrace Beatrice. 'I am grateful for your offer, and so glad that we are close to one another—but I do not wish for a big wedding. Just my family and a few good friends.'

'Captain Denning ought really to speak to Papa,' Beatrice went on after she had returned her embrace. 'But I shall write to him, and you must too, Olivia. Papa can give his consent in writing, and the wedding can be planned for...when? Perhaps in a month's time? Is that too soon? You must tell me what you want, dearest. Do you need more time to get to know Captain Denning?'

'For myself I would marry him tomorrow!' Olivia declared. 'But Jack is coming to discuss the details later this morning.' Olivia laughed as she glanced at the mantel clock. 'If we do not go to bed at once, we shall be sleeping when he calls!'

The sisters smiled at each other in perfect accord.

'I am so happy for you, dearest,' Beatrice said. 'Goodnight then. I wish you sweet dreams, Olivia.'

After her sister had gone, Olivia went to bed and blew out her candle. She closed her eyes as she snuggled down into the feather mattress, but sleep did not come immediately.

Would Jack have proposed to her if they had not been caught in a passionate embrace? Perhaps not quite so soon, but one day surely?

Olivia was aware of a tiny doubt that nibbled at her feeling of happiness. She knew that her reputation would have been severely damaged if Jack had not made it immediately clear that they were engaged. Lady Clements would have seen to that!

Yet surely Jack would not have kissed her in such a way if he did not feel as she did? Olivia understood that gentlemen were not always in love with the ladies they made love to. She knew that Lord Burton had a mistress, and that Lady Burton seemed to accept it as quite normal. But that was another matter, was it not? Their marriage had never been a love match, and they had lived almost separate lives for some years.

Jack must be marrying her because he cared for her. Please God that was so!

She knew that Beatrice and Harry were very much in love, and she was sure that Harry no longer kept a mistress. Beatrice would not have accepted such a situation. Nor would Olivia.

She wanted the kind of marriage her sister had, where the love between them was so strong it could be seen and felt.

Dismissing her foolish doubts, Olivia settled more comfortably in her bed. It was true that Jack had been pushed into making his proposal, but after that kiss he would most likely have done so anyway.

Smiling at her thoughts, Olivia fell asleep.

Chapter Six

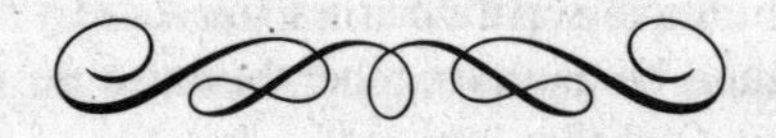

'You know I wish you happy,' Anne said to Jack the next morning. They were walking along the sea-front and had paused to admire the view. 'I am sad that our relationship is over, but it was bound to happen. I am ten years your senior, my dear, and I always knew it would not be a permanent arrangement.' She smiled up at him. ' I do hope we shall continue to be friends.'

'Of course. You know you may always count on me if you need a friend,' Jack said. 'If ever you do need me, Anne, I shall do all I can to help you. I am sorry I was not able to tell you of my decision to marry before the announcement last evening. It happened rather suddenly.'

'These things usually do,' she said with a smile. 'Please do not be anxious on my behalf, Jack. I have been expecting this to happen. Olivia is a lovely girl, both in appearance and nature, and just right for you.'

'She is far above me,' Jack said and frowned. 'I

am not sure that I am the right man for her—she deserves better, Anne—but circumstances have thrown us together, and I shall do my best to make her happy.'

Anne gazed up at him. 'She is a fortunate young woman. Why do you doubt yourself so much? Surely not just because of what occurred at Badajoz? You were unable to prevent what happened that day, Jack, but it was not your fault. You were not to blame because your men ran riot in the streets, nor for what they did that day.'

'They were under my command,' he said, his expression grim. 'I shall never forget that terrible moment when I saw her eyes, Anne. She was screaming, begging me to save her—and I failed.'

'You failed because someone shot you,' Anne said, a spark of anger in her lovely eyes. 'If that ball had entered your skull rather than merely creasing your temple, you would have died. You carry no blame for what happened, my dear.'

'No, perhaps not,' he agreed. 'Had I acted sooner I might perhaps have saved her—but it is not just that, Anne.'

He shook his head as her brows rose in enquiry. Not even to Anne had he been able to unburden himself of the shadows and fears which had haunted him for years, memories that the incident at Badajoz had brought back into sharp focus: memories from his early childhood...of a woman's terrified screams. History had repeated itself, except that in the earlier incident, the woman being raped and beaten was his own mother, and the man raping her was his father, not a pack of blood-maddened soldiers! Badajoz had merely unlocked the nightmare he had banished to a distant corner of his mind, letting the painful memories flood back. Once again, he had been forced to relive that terrible day when the eyes that begged a helpless child for succour had belonged to the mother he adored.

He had run to one of the footmen begging for help for his mother, but the man had laughed and told him the frigid bitch was getting what she deserved. Jack had never forgotten his feelings of despair at not being able to help his mother, and even though she had turned away from him after that day, he had always cared for her.

Anne was speaking again. Jack clamped down on the memories and gave her his attention.

'You should not doubt that your wife will be happy,' Anne said, tucking her arm into his and smiling up at him. 'You are a gentle, good man, Jack Denning, and have often made me happy.' She reached up to kiss his cheek, understanding more than he had ever told her. 'You are not your father, Jack. Do not burden yourself with his sins.'

'How well you understand me.'

They walked on in a companionable silence, until Jack delivered her safely to her brother's house. Neither of them was aware that a man had noticed their actions, a man with jealousy in his eyes and malice in his heart.

'That is settled then,' Beatrice said, smiling at her sister and Jack Denning. 'We shall go ahead with the dance we had planned for next week, but now it will be a special celebration of your engagement. The wedding invitations will be sent out for the second week of August.'

'Will that give you enough time to gather your bride clothes?' Jack asked with a lift of his brows for Olivia.

'Yes, I am sure it will,' she replied, her eyes glowing. 'The seamstress has my details. I shall write to her at once.'

'Then it shall be as you choose.'

'And do you truly need to return to your estates tomorrow?' she asked, an unconscious appeal in her eyes.

'Unfortunately, I do have business that takes me from Brighton,' Jack said. 'But I shall return for our dance, and then I hope to be free to accompany you to your sister's home, and to spend some time with you there.'

Olivia nodded. She wished that he need not leave Brighton at all, but there were only five days before the dance, and they would soon pass.

'Then I shall try to be patient,' she said a little wistfully. 'You must not neglect your business for my sake.'

'Once we are married, we shall have all the time in the world to get to know one another,' Jack said. He turned her hand over to kiss the palm and the look in his eyes set her heart racing like the wind. 'I thought we might travel for a while—to the continent, perhaps Italy? If you would care for it?'

'To Italy?' Olivia stared at him in surprise. 'Could we really do that?'

'I see no reason why not.' Jack laughed. 'And now I must leave you. I have arrangements to make before I leave Brighton.'

'You will dine with us this evening?' Beatrice asked.

'Forgive me, but I cannot,' Jack apologised. 'I have a prior engagement I must keep.'

Olivia was disappointed by his refusal. She had hoped to have a little time alone with her fiancé before his departure, but it was obviously not to be. There was nothing for it but to smile and put a brave face on things. Accompanying him to the door, she gave him her hand to kiss. In her heart, she hoped that he might sweep her up in his arms and kiss her as he had at the ball, but she was disappointed. Jack kissed her hand, gave her another heart-wrenching smile and left.

Olivia sighed. She was happy to be engaged to the man she loved, but something in her was waiting for more—a passionate declaration of undying love perhaps? Her sense of humour came to the rescue, and she smiled at herself. Jack was behaving like a perfect gentleman, and she was a wicked wanton to wish that he would not! It was very wrong of her to want so much more than the chaste kisses he bestowed on her, but she could not help the way her body responded to his merest touch.

Returning to the parlour, she found her sister waiting for her. Beatrice was full of plans for the wedding, and Olivia's disappointment was soon forgotten in the excitement of discussing new clothes and the list of friends whom she planned to invite.

They did not go out that evening, and since most people were feeling a little lethargic after the excitement of the Regent's ball the previous evening, only a few of Beatrice's particular friends came to call. It was not until the following night that Olivia began to receive the congratulations and good wishes of her acquaintances.

They attended a soirée given by Lady Rowlands, and Olivia spent the first part of the evening happily listening to the vocalist and talking with friends. She was about to follow her sister into supper at nine o'clock when she heard her name mentioned by someone close by.

'Naturally he had no choice but to offer,' the sharp, spiteful voice said. 'She set her cap at him from the start, of course, and I dare say he was caught in her toils. But Reginald saw him with his mistress the very next morning. They were embracing. On the promenade! I ask you, is such behaviour decent?'

'Well, what would you expect? I understand it is a

long-standing affair between them, and that he would have married her years ago if she were free. He is hardly likely to…'

Olivia resisted the temptation to glance round. She was well aware that one of the voices belonged to Lady Clements, and refused to give her the gratification of knowing she had been heard. Keeping her head high, she walked on into the supper room, not bothering to listen to the remainder of their gossip. She had obviously been intended to hear their spiteful words. Lady Clements must wish to cause her distress, perhaps to precipitate another broken engagement.

Well, she would be disappointed! Olivia's first reaction was one of anger. She would have liked to inform Lady Clements of exactly what she thought about her schemes! She could not, of course. It would create a terrible scandal. Far better to ignore her, to pretend that she had heard nothing.

Olivia's pride carried her through the rest of the evening with a smile on her lips, though she was a little thoughtful on the carriage ride home.

'Is something wrong, dearest?' Beatrice asked once they were inside the house and alone. 'You seem slightly distant—as if your mind were elsewhere?'

'Nothing is wrong,' she replied and smiled. 'I suppose I am simply missing Jack.'

'Already?' Beatrice teased. 'My poor sister! I do not know what is to become of you if you cannot spend even one day apart, my love.'

Olivia shook her head, refusing to be drawn. She pushed the unpleasant incident from her mind as she went upstairs to undress. She would not dwell on the cruel words of others. Lady Clements had meant to inflict pain because her own plans had gone awry. Olivia would not give her spiteful gossip another thought!

Although it was a while before she succumbed, sleep claimed her at last, and her dreams were so pleasant that she awoke refreshed and more determined than ever not to allow herself to be swayed by gossip or spiteful tongues. She had broken off her engagement to Lord Ravensden because of a jealous girl she had once thought her friend, and though she could not regret having done so, she was determined never to be led into such foolishness again. If she had any reason to believe the tale was true, she would ask Jack for his explanation, she decided, but she had no reason to think ill either of him or of Lady Simmons.

She clung to her determination not to be upset by any fragments of gossip she might hear during the next few days, and, when she met Anne Simmons at a dinner given by a mutual acquaintance, greeted her warmly as the friend she had always been. Let the gossips make what they would of that!

The morning of Olivia's dance arrived. Flowers and gifts were delivered at intervals throughout the day, including some lovely white roses from Jack and a wonderful gift sent by special messenger. Opening the large velvet box, Olivia exclaimed over the beautiful diamond and pearl choker necklace inside.

'How lovely,' Beatrice said when Olivia showed it to her. 'It is just what you need with your new gown. You must wear it this evening, dearest.'

'Yes, I shall,' Olivia replied, her face glowing with happiness. 'Jack asked me to wear it for him.'

His message had been brief but signed with a kiss. Olivia's heart was suddenly racing like the wind, her excitement intense. She could hardly wait for him to come to her.

He arrived half an hour before they were due to leave for the assembly rooms Lord Ravensden had hired for the evening. Beatrice having delayed Harry so that they could be alone for a few minutes, Olivia greeted him in the parlour.

'I am glad to see you safely returned, sir,' she said, a faint flush in her cheeks. 'I hope your business was successful?'

'Jack,' he reminded her, a gleam in his eyes. He took her hand and held it, his eyes going over her with approval. She was wearing a gown of pale lemon silk; it had a high waist, and short sleeves with epaulettes of Italian gauze with a wreath of his white roses at the shoulder. Her hair was caught back from her face with a band of more roses sewn to velvet, and she wore the necklace he had sent around her throat; tiny diamond drops given to her by Beatrice hung from her earlobes. 'My business was tiresome, Olivia. Lawyers, contracts and other matters I would prefer to forget, but necessary I fear. However, I was able to see my mother and acquaint her with my intention to marry. She has sent gifts for you and a letter, which I shall give you tomorrow. She hopes to be at our wedding, but her health will not allow her to travel at the moment.'

Olivia nodded her understanding. 'Perhaps I could make the journey to see Lady Stanhope, to save her the trouble?'

Jack's brow creased in a frown of denial. 'Mama is seeing no one just now. If she is well enough, you will meet her at the wedding. However, my grandfather has indicated that he would like to visit Camberwell prior to the wedding to make your acquaintance. If Lady Ravensden would be prepared to receive him?'

'Yes, of course she would,' Olivia said. 'I am sure Beatrice will be very happy for the Earl to visit us.'

'Then I shall send word immediately.' Jack's frown deepened. 'My father will not attend. As you may have heard, he is dying, albeit slowly.'

Seeing the harsh line of his mouth, Olivia refrained from making any comment, and in another moment the stern expression had gone, replaced by one of his enigmatic smiles that she found so intriguing.

'But I am remiss! You look beautiful, Olivia,' he said, reaching for her hand. 'Allow me, if you please.'

Her heart fluttered as he slid a ring on to the third finger of her left hand. The ring was shaped like a flower, the diamonds beautifully cut and sparkling with a deep fire in the light of the chandeliers.

'It is lovely,' she said, gazing up at him a little shyly. She touched the pendant at her throat. 'Thank you, and for the necklace you sent. You are spoiling me, Jack.'

'You deserve to be spoiled,' he replied, his eyes much warmer now as they rested on her lovely face. 'Olivia, I want to...'

Whatever he had meant to say was lost as the door opened and Beatrice entered, followed by Harry.

'I am sorry to come so soon,' she said, 'but I fear we must be leaving if we are to be ready when our guests begin to arrive.'

'We are quite ready,' Jack said, inclining his head to Lord Ravensden. 'We have some business, sir, but it will keep until tomorrow. I believe you will find my lawyers have prepared the contracts to your satisfaction.'

'I am sure I shall,' Harry replied agreeably. 'But we must not bore the ladies with business. As you said, the morrow will do well enough. And now, we really should be leaving if we are not to be late...'

That evening was to be the happiest Olivia could ever remember. Since everyone knew that it was now her engagement dance, friends and acquaintances fêted her, making a great fuss of her. Many of them had brought small gifts for her, which all added to the excitement. However, it was Jack's behaviour towards her which brought the radiant smile to her face, making her more lovely than ever before.

He was so attentive, so thoughtful, his manner that of a gentleman but also of a lover. They danced together for most of the evening, though some of Olivia's friends did insist on stealing at least one dance, one or two of the gentlemen declaring themselves to be heartbroken. She found a great deal of pleasure in all of this, but it was the way Jack looked at her, the possessive pride in his face as he stood by her to receive the good wishes of their guests, which made her feel so happy.

'You are so lucky,' one of the other young ladies said to her. 'It is obvious that Captain Denning cares for you.'

Olivia only smiled and nodded, but her heart was singing like a lark. Jack's manner had certainly been all that she could have asked that evening, and she could not resist a triumphant glance in Lady Clements's direction. Surely now that lady could not imagine that Jack had a mistress!

Lady Simmons was not at the dance. She and her brother's family had left Brighton the previous day, but she had sent a kind letter and the gift of a silver rose bowl for Olivia.

'I shall hope to be at your wedding,' Anne had written, 'but much depends on my being able to travel.'

Lady Clements's sour look told Olivia that the lady was still feeling annoyed that her nephew had not succeeded in seducing her into an unwanted marriage. She turned away, her head high. It might be that some people would always be ready to whisper spiteful tales, but she did not care for that! She would not allow anything to spoil her happiness.

'My dance, I believe?' Jack swept her away as the musicians struck up the waltz before supper. He looked down at her, his eyebrows raised as if sensing the slight cloud that Lady Clements's sour look had brought to her. 'Is something wrong, Olivia?'

'No, nothing at all,' she replied, giving him a smile that banished all doubts. 'I am very happy.'

'Then that is all I could ask,' Jack said. 'I do pray that you will always be as happy as you are this evening, my love—and that I shall never do anything to cause you grief.'

'I am sure you will not,' Olivia replied. 'Why should you?'

'I would never do so intentionally,' he said, an odd expression in his eyes. 'But should I ever do so, I beg that you will find it in your heart to forgive me?'

'Of course,' she said, a little puzzled by his odd words. 'But if we love each other, all our hurts must be small ones, do you not agree?'

'Yes, you are perfectly right,' he replied and he was smiling again. 'I think a man would have to be a fool indeed if he could not love you, Olivia. You are as lovely inside as out, and that is something rare.'

His compliment left her breathless, all doubts gone in an instant. To say such a thing to her, he must indeed love her with all his heart, and if that was so then nothing else mattered. She was beginning to be aware that there might be a secret in Jack's heart, a secret hurt that had the power to change him from the charming, romantic, teasing man she adored into a brooding stranger. As yet she had no idea what that secret might be, but perhaps when they were married he would find a way to tell her.

'You called me a minx, sir,' she reminded him. 'Can it be that you have changed your mind?'

'No, I have not,' Jack said, the corners of his eyes crinkling with laughter. 'You are indeed a wicked jade, my love, but I shall tame you once we are wed.'

His eyes seemed to promise so much. Olivia's heart beat like war drums, pounding so hard against her ribs that she could scarcely breathe. As she gazed up at him, she saw something in his face that made her long for her wedding night, for the moment she could be truly his.

It was gone in an instant, the teasing, enigmatic expression back as he whirled her round and round the floor to the music, but Olivia held the memory in her heart. If Jack could look at her like that, she had no need to concern herself that he would take a mistress!

They spent two more days in Brighton before leaving for Camberwell, but Jack was with her so often that Olivia's time was filled and she hardly had time to say farewell to her friends. The journey back to

Camberwell was broken once more at the home of Lord and Lady Dawlish, who were very kind to Olivia and her fiancé.

'We shall come to the wedding, of course,' Merry Dawlish told her. 'I would not miss it for the world. Besides, I can never find enough excuses to stay with Harry and Beatrice!'

Once back at Camberwell, Olivia found her father immersed in his project of making the house a warmer place to stay in winter. He greeted her and Jack kindly, gave his permission for their union at once, and promised to return to Abbot Giles to bring Aunt Nan back in time for the wedding.

'I know she will agree it is the best thing for you,' Mr Roade told his daughter. 'You have only to look at Beatrice, my dear. Had your sister been a man she might have been a scholar, made her mark in some profession or other—but she is as happy as a lark wed to Ravensden, and I am sure you will find yourself in much the same situation.'

Olivia smiled and agreed as she kissed her father's cheek. Each day that passed made her more sure that she had been fortunate in her choice of a husband. As they grew more comfortable with each other, they had found much to interest them in each other's company, and she had discovered that Jack shared many of her pleasures, including reading poetry.

'It was often a solace to me in Spain,' he told her once when she had been reading to him aloud from one of her favourite volumes. 'The beauty of a poet's words can sometimes help a wounded soul.'

There had been a look of such sadness in his eyes at that moment! Olivia had longed to reach out and touch his face, to offer her love and understanding, but something made her hold back. Whatever Jack's secret was, she must wait patiently for him to share it with her. Such confidences must not be rushed.

They did not know one another well yet; they had met only a few weeks earlier, though to Olivia it sometimes seemed that she had known him all her life. Indeed, in some ways he was an open book to her. She knew when he found something amusing; their eyes often met in shared appreciation, and she knew he liked to tease her—though not as Harry teased Beatrice. Jack was gentler, more considerate of her feelings. He was a very sensitive, thoughtful man, and she sensed that he had been hurt in the past. She felt very close to him, yet there were times when his thoughts were locked deep inside, and then she had no idea how to reach him.

The Earl of Heggan came to visit two days after they had returned to Cambridgeshire. Olivia found him a little daunting at first, but he was kind and courteous to her, and told her that he was very pleased she was to marry his grandson.

'I had begun to fear that Denning would never marry,' he said, with a glance at Jack. 'I am grateful to you for making him see where his best interests lie, young lady.'

Olivia had sensed that he would have liked to say more to her, but was constrained by the presence of his grandson. She would have liked to talk to him alone, but his visit was brief, no more than two days, and somehow they never seemed to have the chance to talk more intimately.

'I am not sure that I will be able to attend your wedding,' the Earl said before he left. 'But know that my good wishes go with you, my dear. Denning is fortunate in his choice of a bride. I pray that you will both find true happiness together.'

Again, Olivia felt that there was more he wished to say, but perhaps that was merely her imagination? Yet she suspected that Jack had deliberately prevented his grandfather from being alone with her.

After the Earl had gone, she was drawn once more into the whirl of parties and entertainment her sister had arranged for her benefit. Presents and gifts were arriving all the time, though as yet she had not received an answer to her invitation to Lady Burton—or Robina. She presumed that her adoptive mother did not wish to attend, but wondered why her friend had not answered the long letter she had sent her. However, she was too busy to worry about anything very much, allowing herself to forget the tiny doubts that pricked at her now and then. Why should she concern herself over small things when she was to have her heart's desire?

As the days passed and their wedding drew nearer, Jack became more passionate towards her. His kisses were deeper, hungrier, like the one he had given her at the Regent's ball, but he never went too far, never pressed her for more intimate caresses. Olivia knew she would not refuse if he did, but always when she felt herself swooning, wanting his loving to go on, he drew back and smiled at her.

'We have plenty of time,' he whispered once when a moan of frustration escaped her. 'You are mine to cherish, Olivia, and I shall not abuse your trust.'

And so the time passed, and then four days before their wedding Jack was called away.

'I shall see you on the morning of our wedding,' he promised and kissed her lingeringly on the lips. 'Forgive me, dearest, but I must go. I have no wish to leave you, but I fear I have no choice. It seems my father is close to death, and I am called to his bedside.'

Olivia looked at him in surprise. She had understood that nothing would take him back to his father's house. But it was right and natural that he should go.

'Of course you must go,' she said at once. 'Does this mean we may have to postpone the wedding?'

'No, I promise you it does not,' Jack said, touching her cheek gently. 'I shall return in good time, no matter what. My father's death will not change our plans. Indeed, I would not go if he had not sent for me himself. It seems he is in great distress and would make his peace with me. I must go, Olivia, though I had vowed I would never set foot in his house again…but I find that I cannot deny him peace when he is so close to death.'

'Oh, no, you must go to him,' she said at once. 'It would not be right to deny his last request.'

'He does not deserve that I should answer his call,' Jack said, and the bleak, harsh look she had come to dread was back in his eyes. 'But I could not live with my conscience if I ignored his plea.'

'I shall miss you,' she said, gazing up at him. Honesty made her speak out. 'I love you, Jack. I know we were almost pushed into this marriage, but for me it was my heart's desire.'

'Yes, I know,' he said, then bent to kiss her lips. 'I never thought to love, Olivia, but you have become precious to me. Forgive me for leaving you at this time, but I have no choice.'

Olivia smiled and nodded. She clung to him before he left her, feeling as if a shadow had somehow passed across her world, and something inside her made her want to call him back. She felt instinctively that he should not go, and yet decency demanded that he answer his father's call.

After he had ridden away from the courtyard of her sister's home, Olivia stood watching until he had disappeared into the distance. She did not turn until Beatrice came out and called to her, then a shudder ran through her and she felt faint, almost stumbling as she moved to go into the house.

'What is wrong, dearest?' Beatrice asked as she came to steady her. 'You are so pale. Are you ill?'

'No…no, it was just the heat,' Olivia lied. 'It is very warm today, do you not think so?'

'Yes, it is warm,' Beatrice agreed. 'You should not be standing out here in the midday sun. Come into the house, dearest. We do not want you to be ill for your wedding, do we?'

'No, no, of course not,' Olivia said and smiled at her. 'Nothing must spoil the wedding.'

Olivia spent some restless days waiting for Jack's return. One night she lay without sleeping for hours, feeling that he was in some kind of trouble, and that his soul had cried out to hers for comfort, but she told herself she was being fanciful.

She had just finished dressing the next morning when Beatrice walked into her bedchamber. She looked a trifle flustered, which surprised Olivia because her sister seemed to take everything in her stride these days.

'Is something wrong?' she asked. 'You are not feeling unwell? Nothing has happened to the baby?'

'No, indeed I am very well,' Beatrice said. 'I seem to have suffered hardly any morning sickness. It is only that I have this minute received a message from Lady Stanhope. She writes to say she will be unable to attend the wedding as she has received word that her husband is dead.'

'Oh, yes, I see.' Olivia nodded her understanding. 'I knew this might happen, Beatrice. Jack says it will make no difference. He will be here as arranged and the wedding is to go ahead as planned.'

'You are certain?'

'Yes. Jack told me it would not change our plans if his father died.'

Beatrice looked relieved. 'If you are sure, dearest. Lady Stanhope could not come, of course.'

'I do not believe she intended to come,' Olivia said and frowned. 'She sent me gifts as you know, and a kind letter—but I think she never intended to attend the wedding.'

'Surely she must have done?' Beatrice looked at her. 'Why should she not?'

'I do not know, but I have the feeling that Jack did not want her to come.' Olivia blushed as her sister stared at her. 'Perhaps that is foolish of me, but when I offered to visit Lady Stanhope if she was too unwell to travel he was quick to squash the idea.'

'Only because he believed you would meet at the wedding,' Beatrice said. 'Surely there could be no other reason? After all, we received a visit from the Earl of Heggan, and he promised to attend the wedding if he could manage it—though he may not do so now.'

Olivia shook her head but did not attempt to elaborate. Perhaps she had said too much; she might have imagined that reluctance on Jack's part to introduce her to his mother? In any case, she did not wish to discuss the matter further. She believed that, whatever it might be, the mystery lay deep in the past, and was the reason for the shadows in Jack's eyes. One day he might choose to tell her everything, but until that happened, she would not ask.

'I dare say you are right,' she said and kissed her sister on the cheek. 'Do not look so anxious, Beatrice. I am sure I shall meet Jack's mother one of these days.'

They were at supper that evening when the letter was delivered. The housekeeper brought it to Olivia, who opened it and smiled as she looked across the table at her sister.

'It is from Jack,' she said. 'He writes that his father has died and that he will be at Camberwell church in the morning as planned. He says that a quiet funeral was held yesterday at Stanhope, and that his grandfather insists the wedding must go ahead—though he will not be able to attend himself.'

'Then we can be comfortable again,' Beatrice said. 'I wondered if our plans were to be overset at the last moment, but it seems nothing is to be allowed to spoil your wedding, dearest. We must be grateful to the Earl for his concession. I had heard he was a stickler for convention, but this is kind in him, and thoughtful.'

'Yes,' Olivia agreed. She wondered what the Earl had wanted to say to her on his brief visit. 'I thought him a little daunting at our first meeting, but this shows him to have a generous spirit.'

'Yes, indeed.' Beatrice smiled at her. 'So you may

sleep easily tonight, dearest. For tomorrow you shall have your heart's desire.'

Olivia nodded, but made no answer. She was thoughtful as she went to her bed that night, and sleep did not come immediately.

A sense of unease was nagging at her, though she did not know why. Jack's letter had been brief, sent only to reassure her and her sister, and did not mention his feelings. There was no hint that he had missed her, no declaration of love or a hint of his impatience to claim his bride. Olivia was conscious of a nagging doubt. Why should she feel that a shadow had somehow fallen across her happiness?

Nothing had changed, surely? Jack had not been fond of his father. Indeed, she felt that his feelings for Viscount Stanhope came close to hatred. So why should whatever had taken place at Stanhope affect her life? It could not, of course. She was foolish to let her unfounded fears play on her mind, and yet she had the oddest feeling that everything had somehow changed.

Chapter Seven

Jack paused in the act of tying his neckcloth. He was attempting the intricate folds of a Trône d'Amour, but failing miserably under the critical eye of his ex-sergeant. Brett had served as his batman in Spain, now he was both groom and the closest thing Jack had to a valet.

'You'll never do it that way, Captain,' Brett observed. 'You've ruined half a dozen cloths as it is. Best go for something simpler or take it easy. You're in too much of a pother. Not that it's any wonder, being your wedding day and all.'

Jack scowled but did not rebuke his impudence. They were friends. Had it not been for Brett, Jack would probably have died at Badajoz. It was he who had scattered that pack of wolves and had Jack carried back to safety, as he lay unconscious and bleeding from a head wound. Besides, it was not Brett's fault that he was in a foul mood, but entirely Jack's own. He should never have asked Olivia to marry him!

He had been warned enough over the years. Lady Stanhope had told him a thousand times that his father was both mad and evil. The evil he had witnessed for himself on several occasions, but the depth of Stanhope's madness had not revealed itself—at least to Jack!—until the last hours of the Viscount's life.

He carried that man's blood in his veins! The revulsion turned his stomach so that he felt the vomit rise in his throat, bringing a foul taste to his mouth. The madness must always have been there, of course. Some of Stanhope's worst crimes were clearly the product of an unbalanced mind, but he had either cunningly concealed his insanity for years or it had finally overtaken him at the last.

Even before the full extent of his father's madness had been revealed to him, Jack had believed himself tainted. His father had, he knew for certain, killed at least one servant during a brutal beating and maimed others. Had rank, wealth and privilege not protected him, Stanhope must surely have ended at the hangman's noose. As he deserved!

Jack had left Stanhope's house years earlier, vowing never to return. He wished to God that he had not! Wished that he had never seen those wild, staring, bloodshot eyes or the froth of insanity on those drooling lips. Yet even at the end, Stanhope had retained the wits to curse his son with his dying breath.

What to do now? Jack had asked himself the question a hundred times in the past few hours. It would surely be fairer to Olivia if he drew back, for marriage to him might drag her down into the nightmare world he now inhabited. Yet the hurt he must inflict by withdrawing was too terrible to contemplate.

No, no, he could not do such a thing to the woman who had come to mean so much more to him than he had imagined possible. Her reputation would be ruined, her chance of making a good marriage irrevocably damaged. At least as his wife, she would have rank, wealth and the respect of her contemporaries.

'That ain't bad, sir,' Brett remarked, breaking into his thoughts. 'It ain't a Trône d'Amour, nothing like, but it ain't bad. I reckon it will have to do anyways, unless you was thinking of leaving the lady standing at the altar?'

Jack swore softly as he glanced at his gold pocket watch and realised the time. If he had meant to withdraw he had left it too late. He could not destroy Olivia by jilting her so publicly and so cruelly. There was nothing he could do but continue with the wedding.

'You look so beautiful,' Beatrice said, looking at her sister, as she stood dressed in her gown of pure white silk and lace. It was embroidered with little knots of pearls and diamante, and trimmed with silver lace at the hem and on the long, tight sleeves. Olivia's hair was dressed high on her head and caught with white roses and pins of silver set with pearls and diamonds, a little headdress of silk gauze and lace arranged about her hair and then left dangling at the back in long streamers. 'I wish you all the happiness in the world, dearest.'

'If I am as happy as you, I shall be fortunate,' Olivia said and kissed her cheek. 'Thank you for the wonderful gifts you have given me, Beatrice, but most of all for loving me.'

'I have always loved you,' Beatrice said, her eyes bright with tears. 'It broke my heart when the Burtons took you away from us, Olivia. And the way you were treated by them made me angry, but you were brave and honest and the wheel has turned full circle. All I pray now is that you will be able to forget all that has happened to you and live in peace with your husband.' She smiled and touched Olivia's cheek lovingly. 'I know he loves you, dearest. I have seen the way he looks at you sometimes, and so I am convinced that you will be happy.'

'I am sure I shall,' Olivia said. She smiled at her sister, determinedly banishing the foolish fears that had crept into her mind these past days. She too believed that Jack loved her, and she knew that he was more important to her than anything or anyone, even her dearest Beatrice. 'I am so lucky to be marrying him. It is all I want, all I have longed for. I am sure I shall be happy, there is no reason why I should not, is there?'

Beatrice shook her head. The two sisters embraced once more, then went downstairs to where the others were waiting to see Olivia dressed in her bridal gown before setting out for the church.

All the guests had left some time earlier, and the last three carriages carried the bride and her immediate family. A small crowd of well-wishers had gathered in the sunshine to see her arrive at the church, a cheer going up as she went inside on her father's arm.

The lovely old church had been decked with flowers, a profusion of delicate white roses and scented lilies. Ahead of her, Olivia could see the sun streaming through a stained-glass window on to the stone floor in front of the altar, painting the worn flags with a rainbow of colour. Her heart jerked wildly as she saw Jack's tall, commanding figure standing in front of the altar waiting for her, his best man at his side to support him.

Jack turned his head to look as she came to stand by his side, but his expression was stern, unsmiling, and a little shiver of apprehension ran down Olivia's spine. Why did he look so angry? What could she have done to upset him?

She gave him a nervous smile and his expression lightened. He nodded as if to reassure her, but still there was no answering smile, no gesture of greeting to indicate that he had been joyfully anticipating her arrival.

Olivia turned her eyes towards the high altar. She must not allow her imagination to run away with her. There might be many reasons for Jack's withdrawn manner. He might be unwell...or grieving for his father. Sometimes people only realised they loved another person after that person had died. Yes, it might be that, she comforted herself. He could not truly be angry with her.

Olivia answered her vows in a clear, strong voice, and Jack did the same. After the ceremony was over they went into the vestry to sign the register, and Jack seemed more like himself as he shook hands with the vicar. Then they were leaving the church to the sound of pealing bells, the sun pouring down on them as friends and villagers greeted them with laughter and friendly jests. Children came to offer small tokens to Olivia, which she accepted with a smile and a kiss for each child, and then she and Jack climbed into the carriage, which was to take them back to her sister's house.

Olivia glanced at her new husband, half expecting that he would gather her in his arms to kiss her passionately once they were alone, but he made no attempt to do so and she was disappointed by his neglect. Surely he must want to kiss her? She longed to be in his arms, longed for the touch of his lips against hers. He frowned as he saw the invitation in her eyes, then, almost reluctantly, reached for her hand.

'So, Olivia,' he said. 'Does it please you to be Lady Stanhope?'

Olivia looked puzzled, then remembered that he was now the Viscount. She was serious as she looked at him and saw the oddly brooding expression in his eyes.

'I would be as happy to be Mrs Denning,' she said. 'I was sorry to learn of your father's death, Jack.'

'Do not be,' he said, his tone harsh, cold. 'It was the best for all concerned.'

Olivia felt slightly hurt by his tone but concealed it. Something was obviously troubling him, but it seemed it was not his father's death. What had caused this strange mood? Olivia knew of nothing that could have made him withdraw from her...unless he had begun to regret his promise to marry her?

'Do not look so anxious,' Jack said, as if reading her thoughts. 'We are married now for good or ill, and I shall do my best to make your life happy, no matter what.'

Olivia could not answer him. Her throat ached and her chest felt tight as the disappointment swept over her. Had she been wrong to think he loved her? Before that visit to his father's house, he had seemed to feel passion towards her. Now he was distant, polite, considerate, but remote. Why had he changed towards her? What could she have done to make him look at her like that? It was almost as if he were horrified at finding himself bound to her in marriage. Yet perhaps that was merely Olivia's imagination playing tricks on her?

The carriage had drawn up outside Camberwell House, and Jack jumped down, giving her his hand to help her down. Olivia smiled at him, concealing her heartbreak. Her pride would not allow her to show her hurt, either to him or to her friends.

Throughout the reception, she kept her smile in place, laughing and chattering to her guests as though she was the happiest woman alive—which she would be if only she could rid herself of the fear that Jack was regretting their marriage.

Surely he would have told her if he had decided he could not love her after all? He had spoken of love only a few days earlier, now he was behaving almost like a stranger. Had something occurred which had made him wish he had not promised to marry her? The thoughts went round and round in her head like a spinning-top.

It was just before she was due to go upstairs and change into her travelling-gown that Lady Clements came up to her. She was looking oddly satisfied, her mouth curved in a smile that was wholly false.

'Such shocking news,' she said, tapping Olivia's arm with her gloves. 'One might have imagined he would live for years…but such is the way of life. These accidents happen so suddenly, and then everything is changed.'

'Do you speak of Lord Stanhope?' Olivia asked, feeling puzzled. 'I understood his death had been long expected.'

'No, my dear, of course not,' Lady Clements replied, licking her lips rather like a cat who has just devoured the cream. 'It was of Lady Simmons's husband I was speaking. A riding accident, they say. He fell from his horse and broke his neck.'

'Oh, how terrible,' Olivia said at once. 'Anne did promise to be here today if she could, but now I understand why she could not manage it. It is very shocking for her.'

'I dare say she does not care so very much,' Lady Clements replied sourly. 'I dare say she would have divorced him long since if her family would have permitted it. She will do better as a widow, though I believe I should be right in thinking she regrets that the accident did not set her free a few weeks earlier.'

Olivia felt the colour draining from her face. The tone of Lady Clements's voice left her in no doubt of her meaning. Oh, how could she imply such a thing? It really was too bad of her.

'I know Lady Simmons well enough to be sure that she would never hope for anyone's death,' she replied, 'and particularly not the father of her children.'

'You are very loyal to your friends,' the older woman said. 'Let us hope that your loyalty is not misplaced, Lady Stanhope.'

Olivia did not reply, merely turning away as her sister came up to her. She had not wished to invite Lady Clements to the wedding, but Beatrice had said they must, because the family was distantly connected to Harry's.

'Are you ready to go up, dearest?' Beatrice asked.

'Yes, quite ready,' Olivia said and smiled at her.

She would not let that woman's poisoned barbs hurt her! Olivia followed her sister from the reception room, her progress slowed by the wishes of friends who wished to say goodbye to her. Their kindness soothed her frayed nerves, and she had almost managed to dismiss the incident by the time she reached her bedchamber.

Beatrice and one of the maids helped Olivia take off her lovely wedding-gown. She had decided on a plain dress of pale green silk for travelling, with a darker green redingote shot through with silver thread. She wore a village hat, the brim turned up in front and behind and the crown shaped into a little dome with a festoon of ribbons and silk roses round it, which looked very fetching.

'You look beautiful,' Beatrice assured her. 'Jack must be very proud of his bride.'

'I am sure he is,' Olivia replied, giving her sister a naughty look. She had decided to ignore all her doubts and fears, and she did not intend that Beatrice should guess she was uneasy. 'I am very proud of him.'

'As well you should be,' Beatrice replied. 'Go down to him now, my love. I dare say he is impatient to be on his way.'

'Yes, I dare say he is,' Olivia said and smiled as she kissed her sister's cheek. 'I do not know where he plans to take me now, though he has spoken of travelling to Italy.'

'I should imagine you will spend a little time at his estate first,' Beatrice said, 'so that you can become accustomed to your new home, and to each other. You must write to me soon, Olivia, and tell me all your news.'

'Yes, of course I shall,' Olivia said. She resisted

the temptation to cling to her sister. Beatrice was in a delicate condition; she must not be burdened with Olivia's troubles. Besides, all these foolish doubts and fears might be for nothing. 'Take care of yourself, dearest. I shall look forward to seeing my niece or nephew when the child is born.'

They went back downstairs together. There was a flurry of farewells, hugs and kisses from her papa and Nan, and a kiss on the cheek from Harry.

'Take care of her, Stanhope,' he said. 'We shall expect you to visit us at Christmas. Beatrice will not be able to travel by then, and I know she will want to see her sister.'

Jack inclined his head in assent, but his smile and manner of taking leave was formal. He insisted on helping Olivia into the carriage himself, but after enquiring if she was quite comfortable, leaned back against the velvet squabs on the seat opposite and stared at a point above her head.

Everything went off well, did you not think so?' Olivia asked after a moment. 'Was the reception to your liking, sir?'

'Yes, of course. Lady Ravensden is an excellent hostess,' Jack replied. 'We could not have asked for more.'

'Your friend Viscount Gransden was very pleasant,' Olivia observed, determined to break down this barrier of silence. 'He spoke to me kindly at the reception, and he sent us some very fine oriental vases, you know.' She paused, but as he made no comment she went on. 'The Earl of Heggan sent a wonderful silver tea and coffee service as well as a set of Sèvres tea bowls and a complete dinner and dessert service. Beatrice has displayed all the gifts in the long gallery and will send them on to us. Is the Viscount a particular friend of yours?'

'Grandfather gave me the Heggan jewels for you. I will give them to you later,' Jack said, frowning slightly as she paused, clearly inviting him to comment. 'As for Leander Gransden, he is a decent enough fellow. We have been friends for years, though I had not seen him since I joined the army. He is his father's heir and the Marquis would not permit him to come to Spain with me, for fear that he should be killed.'

'You are the heir to the Earl of Heggan's title, are you not?'

'In my case it was different,' Jack said harshly. 'I do not care for titles, which is as well since they are destined to die with me.'

'Surely not…' Olivia stopped and blushed as she saw Jack's look. His eldest son would be the heir to both the Stanhope and Heggan titles—unless, of course, he meant to renounce them. Would he do that? Olivia wondered. It would make no difference to her. She cared little whether she was known as my lady or madam.

'Do not be anxious,' Jack said. 'We shall talk about these things later, Olivia. We have plenty of time ahead of us.'

But she wanted to talk! She wanted to know what had brought that bleak expression back to his eyes.

'Where are we going?' she asked, since he was clearly unwilling to make conversation himself.

'To my estate at Briarwood for the moment,' Jack replied. 'Circumstances have changed, Olivia. I had made plans for the future, but now I must think. I crave your forbearance. Forgive me if I seem preoccupied. You must and shall know all, but I need a little time to decide what to do for the best.'

Olivia bit back the questions that were ready to tumble off her tongue. It was very clear to her that Jack was deeply troubled in his mind, but for the moment he was not prepared to share his thoughts with her.

'Yes, of course,' she replied. She dare not look at him as she added, 'I heard from Lady Clements that Anne Simmons is now a widow.'

'That woman is a spiteful witch,' Jack said and scowled. 'You should ignore her, Olivia. You have nothing to fear. Our marriage may have been hasty, but I hope nothing I do in the future will cause you unnecessary grief. You may look forward to all the respect and attention Lady Stanhope is entitled to expect from me.'

His declaration should have reassured her, but it was so formal. He had hardly touched her, except to hold her arm or her hand for a brief moment. She had expected something very different from the man who had kissed her so passionately at the Regent's ball.

His odd manner sent a chill down her spine. Surely he would not speak so if he were the eager bridegroom she had expected? What had happened to make him withdraw? Had she been mistaken in his feelings towards her? Or was it only now that Lady Simmons was free that he had begun to regret his promise to Olivia?

It was late before they reached the inn where they were to stay for the night. Olivia was too tired to feel hungry and ate only a few mouthfuls of the supper brought to the parlour Jack had hired for them.

'You are exhausted,' Jack said, and for a moment the barrier was down and she saw something in his eyes that made her heart beat faster. 'I shall escort you to your room, Olivia.'

'My room?' she asked. Her eyes were dark with hurt as she gazed up into his face, searching for a sign that he truly cared for her. 'Will you not join me, Jack?'

'Not this night,' he told her, his own eyes seeming to be looking somewhere far beyond her. 'We married in haste, Olivia. You should more fairly have been courted for months before we became engaged. I am in no hurry to claim a husband's rights. It is better that we get to know one another for a while.'

Olivia felt her cheeks grow warm with embarrassment. She must seem like a wanton hussy to him, begging for his attentions! Yet his kisses had given her the impression that he was impatient to make her his own, and she could not understand why he no longer wanted her—unless he was in love with Anne Simmons.

It seemed the most likely explanation. Olivia blinked to hold back the stupid tears, which threatened to fall and shame her. She refused to cry or to show her hurt!

Her head went up as pride came to her rescue and she felt a flicker of anger. If he had wanted to marry Anne, he should have told her the truth, he should have been honest with her. She would have released him from his promise, of course she would. Yet at the start he had believed Anne would never be free to marry him, and perhaps he had thought it too cruel to jilt Olivia at the last moment.

Surely this was even crueller. To be married to a man she adored who did not love her was hardly bearable!

At the door of the inn's best bedchamber, she turned to him; her bearing was proud and dignified as she looked into his face and saw that closed expression once more shutting her out.

'Then I shall wish you goodnight, sir,' she said. 'I hope your dreams will be pleasant ones.'

'I have little expectation of it,' Jack said, a rueful smile in his eyes. He reached out and took her hand, raising it to kiss it. 'Forgive me, Olivia. I beg you, do not hate me just yet. You may hate me when I tell you what I must, but I pray you will find it in your heart to forgive me one day.'

'Jack, what is it?' she asked, suddenly sensing the anguish he had been fighting all day. 'Please—will you not tell me?'

'In time,' he said. 'In truth, I do not know my own mind as yet, Olivia. I am lost, wandering in a maze from which I fear there is no escape. I would extricate myself and come to you, sweet, lovely Olivia, but it might bring terrible harm to you. That is the one thing I am determined shall never be, though it cuts the heart from me to hurt you, as I must.'

Olivia stared as he turned and walked away from her. There was much more here than she had guessed. Perhaps his changed manner was due not to Lady Simmons's bereavement but to something else entirely?

She kept her tears at bay as she went into the bedchamber and allowed her maid to undress her, then dismissed her, ignoring the girl's simpering smiles. No doubt Rosie imagined she was about to fall into the arms of her eager husband instead of retiring to a lonely bed.

Olivia lay awake for some time pondering the mystery of Jack's odd behaviour, but she could not even begin to understand what lay behind those cryptic words.

If he truly loved her, as his last words surely implied, then why was he holding back? Why did he not come to her and claim her as his own?

'Here we are then, Briarwood House,' Jack said as he helped Olivia from the carriage. 'I am sorry you are seeing your new home for the first time on a wet day, Olivia. It is not the most handsome of residences, though stoutly built and comfortable. Sir Joshua was a country gentleman, not given to fancy ways. However, now that you are mistress here, you may wish to make changes. Please be assured that I shall leave all such matters in your hands. You may spend what you wish, employ the services of any craftsman you think fit.'

Despite his careless words, it was a fine house with many windows. The walls were built of grey stone and covered with creeping ivy, which softened and beautified its austerity.

'I hope you will be happy here.'

Olivia nodded and smiled but gave him no reply. The last stage of their journey here had been very much easier. Jack had made some effort to converse normally after that first evening, when he had left her at the door of her bedchamber. He had even complimented her on her appearance, and teased her a little about a particularly pretty bonnet. He was polite, considerate, attentive, but distant. They might have been mere acquaintances instead of bride and groom.

'Ah, here are Jenkins and Mrs Jenkins to greet you, Olivia.' He turned to the elderly couple who had brought the servants into the front hall to greet them. 'May I present Lady Stanhope. Mrs Jenkins, my wife is tired from the journey. Please show her the apartments you have prepared for her comfort.'

'Yes, my lord.' The housekeeper curtsied to him and then to Olivia. 'May I say that you are very welcome here, milady. We are all very pleased to see you at Briarwood.'

Olivia thanked her and asked to meet the maids and footmen who were lined up to greet her. She smiled at each one in turn, repeating their names so that she would remember them, then she followed Mrs Jenkins up the stairs and along the hall.

Despite what Jack had said about the house not being grand, Olivia saw that it was quite substantial and well-furnished, with at least ten bedrooms besides the master suite to which she was shown. This consisted of a sitting-room, and a large bedchamber with a dressing-room that connected to another bedroom.

'This was once Sir Joshua's room,' Mrs Jenkins informed Olivia as she opened each door in turn. 'Captain Denning…or his lordship as I should properly say now…used another room when he was here before, but he instructed that we were to open the master suite ready for you, milady.'

Her own rooms were decorated in shades of primrose, pale greens and white, but Jack's was crimson and gold and seemed a little dark. Olivia thought that had circumstances been otherwise between them, she would have liked to change things here, make them brighter, with new drapes about the bed and at the windows.

'Yes, I see,' Olivia said. 'It all looks very welcoming, Mrs Jenkins. I am sure we shall be comfortable here, thank you.' Returning to her own bedchamber, she saw that a bowl of white roses had been placed on the dressing-chest. 'Oh, those are lovely. I can smell their perfume from here.'

'Yes, they do have a powerful perfume,' the housekeeper replied with a smile. 'They grow in the walled garden, milady. There are nearly always roses growing in the sheltered spots right up until Christmas. His lordship asked me to bring you some every day they are in flower.'

'How thoughtful of him,' Olivia said, tears stinging her eyes. 'I do love roses, and these have such a wonderful scent.'

'I shall leave you to refresh yourself now,' the housekeeper said. 'If you need anything else, you have only to ring.'

'Thank you, I am sure I shall not need you for the moment. I will come down and have tea in the parlour in half an hour.'

'Yes, milady.'

Mrs Jenkins went away, and Olivia began to explore her rooms. They might not be grand, but there was everything a lady could need for her comfort. A pretty writing-desk fashioned of rich mahogany and inlaid with bands of different coloured woods stood by the window. She went over to it, discovering that the drawers contained notepaper, silver-handled pens, inkpots and a leather-bound blotter with the initials OD inscribed in silver. Jack must have had it made for her especially before his father's death created him Lord Stanhope.

As she moved around the sitting-room, she noticed other items which looked new, as if Jack had thought hard about what his bride might need. The rooms had obviously belonged to Sir Joshua's wife, and some of the original furniture had been retained. These pieces were rather lovely, like the footstool, which looked as if the lady of the house might have covered it herself. The pretty stitching enchanted Olivia. She spent some minutes examining the tapestry, then moved on to a delicate cabinet containing figurines made in the Derby porcelain factory. There was also an embroidery frame, a needlework box with a profusion of silks, and a spinet, as well as various tables, display cabinets and a daybed covered in green silk brocade.

The bookcase was new, and Olivia was thrilled to discover on its shelves some of her favourite poets, together with many she did not know. Various silver trinkets had her name engraved on them, and all the hangings were embroidered with her initials.

Olivia could not doubt that when Jack had given instructions for these rooms to be prepared for her, he had been eagerly anticipating the coming of his new bride. So why had he withdrawn from her now?

She could not think that she had done anything to displease him. Indeed, his manner would seem to indicate otherwise. He was kind and considerate towards her, and she had sometimes seen an oddly tortured expression in his eyes, as though he was deliberately holding himself on a tight rein. She had begun to think that whatever was disturbing him had nothing to do with Olivia herself. Something must have happened at Stanhope.

Olivia had always sensed a mystery in Jack's past: something so powerful and terrible that it could bring a haunted expression to his dark eyes. He had been struggling against his fears when she first met him, but when they met again in Brighton he had seemed to conquer them, to become a very different man. Now the darkness in his past had reached out to claim him once more.

But it should not claim him! As she tidied her gown and prepared to go downstairs, Olivia found herself drawing on reserves of strength she had never realised she possessed.

She would not let Jack slip away into that world of shadows and pain, where he was haunted by the secrets of the past. Somehow she would find a way to bring him back to her! She would make him laugh and look at her with desire, and she would make him love her.

'I love you too much,' she whispered. 'I cannot let you go, Jack. We are married, and I shall be your true wife one day. I shall find a way to make you love me. I swear it…'

Chapter Eight

'So, Olivia,' Jack said as she joined him in the parlour before dinner that evening. 'Are you satisfied with your house? Shall you be comfortable here?'

'Yes, I am certain I shall,' Olivia replied and gave him one of her most bewitching smiles. 'It is a charming house, Jack: a real family home. I like it very well, though of course I have not yet seen all the rooms. Mrs Jenkins is to take me over it in the morning so that I can assess it properly—unless you have other plans for us?'

'No, no, you must do just as you please,' he said, a flicker of amusement in his eyes. 'Do you mean to change much, my dear?'

She caught the teasing note in his voice and laughed, a feeling of relief sweeping over her. Perhaps his odd mood was beginning to ease.

'Oh, do not fear that I mean to make you uncomfortable, Jack. I dare say I shall not change so very much—though I believe your own bedchamber needs new drapes. You will not mind that, I hope?'

'No, I shall not mind,' he said, and for the first time since their wedding day he was more like the man she had known in Brighton and at Camberwell. 'Indeed, I have thought the whole house could do with refurbishing. Sir Joshua did not bother much after his wife died. She was a lovely woman and I know he mourned her for the rest of his life. I believe he lived only for his work in later years.'

'Mrs Jenkins showed me her portrait,' Olivia said. 'She had a gentle face and kind eyes.'

'Should we have your portrait drawn, Olivia?'

'Only if your likeness is taken at the same time, so that our portraits may hang side by side.'

'But I should make a poor subject for the artist, whilst you are beautiful.'

'Thank you.' Olivia dimpled at him. 'If I am honest, I thought you less than attractive at our first meeting, sir—but you have improved in looks a little these past weeks.' Her eyes were alight with mischief as she went on, 'Though I dare say you will never be the most handsome of men.'

'I thank you, my lady wife.' Jack laughed, much amused by her honesty. 'You are very complimentary.'

'Oh, I did not mean to compliment you,' replied Olivia, pretending innocence. 'It is always best to be open in these matters. Do you not agree? Besides, I did not marry you for your looks, my lord.'

'Indeed?' Jack raised his brows. 'May I ask why you did marry me?'

'Because when you kissed me I felt something no other man had ever made me feel,' she said. 'Had you asked, I would have been yours that night. I want to be yours in every sense. It is my right, Jack.'

'Olivia…' The colour left his cheeks. He looked stunned by her frankness. 'Please…you do not know what you ask.'

She moved towards him, gazing up into eyes that were black with anguish. 'I only ask that you should care for me a little, that we should share the pleasures of a husband and wife. Is that so very much, Jack?'

Jack drew in a ragged breath. She could sense the emotions raging inside him as he hesitated, then, as she reached up to stroke his cheek, he jerked back as though her touch would burn him. Turning away from her, he crossed the room to stand by the window. She thought he had needed to put distance between them, as if he could not quite trust himself to be near her.

'We shall be friends,' he said at last, and the words were forced from him. 'Everything I have is yours, Olivia. My fortune, my home, my devotion—but that is all I can give you.'

'Why so?' she cried. 'I love you, Jack. My heart is yours already, as you well know. Why will you not take all that I would offer you? We are wed and there is no sin in seeking pleasure together.'

He turned then and she saw that his features were contorted with the pain and anguish she had sensed hidden these past two days. 'Do not ask that of me,' he said, his voice husky with emotion. 'If you do, I must leave this house tonight.'

'No!' she cried, terrified by something she felt but did not understand. He was desperate, clinging on by the finest of threads. 'I beg you, do not leave me here alone. It would break my heart. Please stay with me, Jack.'

'I fear our hearts will break whether I go or stay,' Jack said, and crossed the room in strides to stand before her. His expression was grave as he gazed down at her. 'I must struggle alone with this for the moment. Give me three months to reach a decision, Olivia. I shall leave no stone unturned in my efforts to free us from this nightmare. At the end of that time I promise to explain everything.'

Olivia met his anguished look, and wished that she might somehow help to bear his pain. 'And during that time we shall be friends? You will not keep a barrier between us?'

'Only that I must,' he said his voice husky with emotion. 'Can you bear it, Olivia? Be just my friend? Believe that I would rather have died at Badajoz than cause you a moment's pain?'

He loved her! Olivia believed in that moment that Jack loved her more than she could ever have imagined. She could not know what had caused him to draw back, to deny his feelings, but she did know that he was finding it painful—that he wanted her as much as she wanted him. Her heart lurched. She would never let him go. She would break down this barrier between them somehow!

Her eyes held his, demanding honesty from him.

'You were badly hurt at Badajoz, I think. Can you not tell me what happened there?'

Jack hesitated, then inclined his head in assent. 'Yes, you are entitled to at least that.'

His eyes stared into the distance as his mind was transported back to the heat and dust of an old Spanish town. The stench of blood and death had soaked into the cobbles that day, the dark, narrow streets strewn with debris from the battle. Jack had been making a reconnoitre of the situation when he came upon that terrible scene.

He saw it now, as clearly as if it were happening that moment. A woman caught at the steps of a church. Clearly she had thought to find sanctuary within its ancient walls, but the soldiers had surrounded her. Maddened by the heat and the bloodlust of battle, they were like a pack of dogs baying at a wounded doe.

The woman had looked at Jack, a desperate appeal in her liquid brown eyes. She was young, perhaps no more than twenty, a peasant girl with long curling hair. He had seen blood on her arms and face, the torn shreds of her bodice revealing her full breasts.

'God damn the lot of you,' Jack had cried. 'I command you to stop. Let this woman go free!'

He had never known from whence came the ball that creased his temple and laid him low, but the next moment he was lying face down on the earth. Still conscious, he had tried to struggle to his feet, cursing and threatening to hang the pack of them, and then something had smashed against the back of his head and he had fallen into the dark pit of unconsciousness, where he had remained for several days.

Olivia listened in silence to Jack's story. She sensed that it had caused him some anguish in the telling, and thought she could begin to see why he sometimes seemed haunted by his memories.

'They raped her,' Jack ended hoarsely. 'She was no older than you, Olivia. I have been told that she fought them to the last—and in the end they killed her. She was not the only one to suffer that day. Our men behaved disgracefully, raping and plundering the homes of innocent citizens…women and children died for their greed and bloodlust.' His face was grey with exhaustion, as though it had cost him much to relive the ordeal.

'But you tried to save her,' Olivia said softly.

'Tried and failed.'

'You carry no blame for what those soldiers did,' she said. 'I have read in the history books that these things sometimes happen, though I know it is terrible and must cause shame to fall on those who become as beasts in the heat of the moment. But you were not one of them, Jack. I respect you for what you attempted. It was brave and honourable.'

She was standing so close! Her perfume was in his nostrils, stirring his senses, making him ache with the desire to know her intimately, to carry her to his bed and make her his own.

'Olivia…' His hand moved of its own volition, his fingers trailing her cheek. 'If only I…'

She believed that he wanted to kiss her. He was fighting himself. Her lips parted invitingly as she smiled up at him, sensing that he was close to losing his battle.

'Dinner is ready, milord.'

The spell was broken as Jenkins spoke from behind them. Jack blinked rapidly, seeming to wake from a trance. He stepped back from her, the iron control once more in place.

'Thank you, Jenkins. We shall come at once.' As he turned to Olivia, his expression was once more that of a polite stranger. He offered her his arm. 'If you please, my dear. I understand Cook has prepared something special for your first evening. It would be discourteous of us to keep her waiting.'

Olivia stood patiently as Rosie helped her into her filmy night-chemise, but dismissed her as soon as the girl had gathered up the gown she had worn earlier.

'Thank you, you may retire now,' she said. 'I shall not need you again this evening.'

She stared into the mirror as the maid went away, then picked up her brush to smooth her hair into a cloud of silken strands that fell on her shoulders in a shining mass. As a child Olivia had loved to have her hair brushed by Lady Burton, but now she preferred to do it herself.

Laying down the brush, Olivia sighed. Was she never to find peace? She had hoped for so much from her marriage, and now…what? Jack's moods puzzled her. They seemed to come and go, as if he sometimes managed to rise above whatever haunted him, but he had only to look at her to be cast down again.

What was it that haunted him? Why was he so determined to hold back from her? She could not begin to guess, but she was determined to overcome his resistance somehow.

She rose from her stool and began to walk about her bedchamber, pausing to sniff the delicate perfume of the roses Jack had sent her. He was so thoughtful, and he had asked her to be his friend. Well, she would be that, of course, but she would also be much more one day.

A smile touched her lips as she thought of something. Going over to her writing desk, she took out a sheet of notepaper and wrote a few words on it, signing it with the initials OD and a kiss. After a moment's thought, she sprinkled two drops of her perfume on to the notepaper. She then selected a perfect bud from the roses and went through into Jack's bedchamber. He had not yet come up. Olivia had suspected as much. She had left him relaxing with a glass of brandy in the parlour, and thought he meant to sit on for a while.

Was he restless? Was he thinking of her? Well, she

would make him aware of her lying next door whether he wished it or not! She laid her note and the rose on Jack's pillow, then went back into her own room and softly closed the door.

It might be that Jack's resistance would take a long time to overcome, but she would find a way. No matter how often he repulsed her, she would not let him slip away. Somehow she knew that the future happiness of them both depended on her having the strength to hold him despite himself.

Downstairs, alone in the parlour, Jack stared moodily at his glass. He had already drunk more than was usual for him and the fiery spirit had done nothing to ease the ache inside him. His mind was filled with images of Olivia, with the smell of her skin and the sound of her voice.

Damnation! He must put the images from his mind or he would go mad in truth. He had not realised how hard this would be for either of them when he decided to go through with this marriage—a marriage that must forever be in name only.

He could not claim his lovely bride. She would be tainted by his touch, and she was so lovely, so pure—so far above him!

Besides, there was the matter of a child. As yet, the madness had never shown itself in any shape or form in Jack, but for years Stanhope had managed to conceal his own insanity from the world. It might be that the sickness would never show itself in Jack, but he could not be certain that it would not recur in his son. To protect that unborn child and Olivia from such horror, he knew that he must resist the urgings of his flesh.

Better that he should suffer a thousand torments than that his touch should defile Olivia. For he loved her desperately. At first he had been merely caught by her naughty smiles, but her bravery and her honesty had won respect from him. He knew now without a shadow of a doubt that he had found a rare jewel in the woman he had taken to wife.

The pain washed over him in waves. He was torn with remorse and anguish for the hurt he was causing Olivia. She deserved so much more than he could give her.

He had thought by marrying her to save her from the slights of others, but now he understood that she would have been strong enough to bear the cruel gossip and scandal which would have resulted from her being left at the church. What he had done was far worse!

He had robbed her of the chance to love and be loved, of the chance of having a child.

What could he do to make amends? Jack was tormented by the knowledge that nothing he could give Olivia would replace what he had stolen from her by marrying her under false pretences.

Why had he done it? Was it truly only to save her from the humiliation of being jilted? Or was there another darker reason? Had he followed his own selfish desires? His honesty forced him to admit that he wanted her for his own. Even now, his flesh burned for her. His senses screamed out that he should go to her, make her his own.

No, no, he could not, must not give way to his selfish desires!

He should ride away this very night, give Olivia grounds for an annulment…yet even as the thought came into his mind he dismissed it. He did not want to give her up. Being with her tore him apart, but he had not the strength to leave her.

She had played for him that evening, singing popular ditties in her clear, high voice, some of which were a little wicked and had made him raise his brows at her. If he left her now there would be little chance of either of them finding happiness. Olivia would not marry again; he knew it instinctively, as he knew there could never be another woman for him.

There must be a way out of this dilemma! Jack had been going over and over the situation in his mind. Perhaps if he were careful, if he could make certain that there was never a child…but he would need to tell Olivia the truth. He could not deceive her. How would she feel if he told her that there was a chance her husband might descend into madness? Would she turn from him in horror? Surely she would hate him for what he had done to her?

Yet if Stanhope's madness had come upon him for another reason…perhaps some foul disease had rotted his brain? If he could be sure that there was no danger of the sickness being passed on through Jack's blood…

Damn the man who had given him life! Anger and hatred stirred in his breast. His father had never once shown him affection. Nor if he were truthful had his mother. Servants had cared for Jack all his life, only Sir Joshua making the attempt to know him—though perhaps the Earl had done so once.

There had been an occasion when the Earl had found him playing in the garden with a wooden sword. He had asked if Jack wanted to be a soldier. He had smiled and touched the boy's head gently…and then Lady Stanhope had come and the Earl had turned away, his face an impassive mask once more.

Jack dismissed the memory. It could not matter now. The Earl had lied to him by omission all these years. He should have told Jack the truth about this curse long since.

Jack was angry with his grandfather. Why had the Earl told him it was his duty to marry for the sake of the family? Surely it was better that the madness should die with Jack?

The tortured thoughts went round and round in his mind as he abandoned his glass, the remains of the golden liquid still clinging to the sides, and made his way up to his bedchamber. He paused outside the door, hesitating before going inside. It might be better if he were to use his old rooms, yet that would be to insult Olivia…to make her the butt of the servants' jokes.

No, he would not offer her more slights. Besides, what difference if there was but one door between them or several? He would suffer as much if he were a thousand miles hence!

Jack went inside, then stiffened. Her perfume was stronger here than it had been in the parlour. Had she been here? His eyes were drawn towards the bed and the rose that lay on his pillow. Frowning, he crossed the room in quick strides, snatching up both note and rose.

'Sweet dreams, my friend,' Olivia had written. 'I shall dream of you, dearest Jack.'

Jack was torn between laughter and tears. She was indeed the minx he had named her! If only he could go through that door and claim her as his own. He moved towards the door that led through to her bedchamber, his thoughts feverish with longing.

No! No, he would not give into his carnal desires! That would be a wicked act, to destroy the woman he would honour above all others. He was strong enough to resist her. And if the time came when he could not, he must leave her.

Cursing softly, Jack turned the key locking the door that separated them. There must be no surprise visits from Olivia, for if he were to wake and find her lying by his side he did not think he would be strong enough to send her away.

* * *

'I believe you have seen everything now, milady,' Mrs Jenkins said the following morning after an extensive tour of the house. 'If you wish to make changes with the way things are run, you have only to say. Sir Joshua left most things to me.'

'And so shall I,' Olivia replied with a smile. 'I may make small changes from time to time, but I have never had the charge of a house such as this, Mrs Jenkins. I shall rely on you to tell me how things ought properly to be done.'

'Yes, milady. You may rely on me.' The housekeeper looked well pleased. 'Those cream drapes we discovered will go beautifully around the four-poster bed in his lordship's chamber. I shall have the maids hang them directly.'

'Yes, please do. I shall come up later to see how they look.'

Olivia left the housekeeper to go about her business and made her way to the pretty parlour at the back of the house, which she had decided to make her own. It had long French windows leading out on to the lawns and the rose gardens. She opened them and went out, feeling pleased that the weather had brightened considerably. There was no sign of rain, and the sun was beginning to peep through the clouds.

She began to walk about the gardens, pausing to inhale the perfume of a dark red bloom, then stiffened as she heard a low growling noise.

The dog was staring at her suspiciously, not bristling with rage as it had in the woods the day she had first seen Jack, but uneasy and ready to pounce if she made a wrong move. Olivia took a deep breath as she told herself not to panic. What had Jack called the beast? Ah yes, she remembered now.

'Sit, Brutus!' she said in a tone of command. 'Good dog. Sit!'

To Olivia's absolute amazement, Brutus obeyed instantly. She stared at him for a moment or two, hardly daring to breathe. What ought she to do now? Would he spring up to impede her passage if she walked away?

This just would not do! Olivia realised that she had no choice but to establish a relationship with the dog. She simply could not allow Brutus to make her a prisoner of the house. Somehow she must conquer her nerves.

Someone had once told her that she should never show an animal fear, and she believed it was true. Gathering her courage, she took a few steps towards the dog. Brutus growled low in his throat but remained in the sitting position she had commanded him to assume.

'Good boy,' Olivia murmured, encouraged by his apparent obedience. She moved closer, finally coming to a halt inches from the dog's nose. 'I am not a gypsy, Brutus. I am your master's wife. We should be friends. We have his best interests at heart, do you not agree?'

Brutus looked at her uncertainly, then wagged his

tail slightly. Olivia relaxed as she saw he was inclined to be friendly.

'What a good dog you are,' she said, then daringly held her hand out for him to smell. He sniffed a couple of times, then licked her. Olivia smiled and bent down to caress his head, tickling him behind the ears, something he seemed to like very much if the way his tongue lolled out was anything to the point. 'Yes, you are a good boy,' she said. 'Would you like to come for a walk with me?'

Brutus recognised the word and barked, but the sound was joyful and not in the least hostile.

'Yes, you would like a walk,' Olivia said, adopting the tone people normally reserved for puppies and small children. 'I dare say you have been waiting for ages for someone to take pity on you. Come along then, and afterwards we shall ask Mrs Jenkins for a nice bone for you.'

Brutus barked his agreement and set off in front of her. He was a large dog and exuberant, but seemed to have accepted Olivia as his friend, running a few yards ahead of her and then returning. When he picked up part of a fallen branch and brought it to her, Olivia instantly understood what he wanted and took it from him, throwing it as hard as she could.

'Fetch!' she cried. 'Good dog, fetch!'

Brutus obeyed without hesitation. Olivia laughed, her fear of the huge hound disappearing as he deposited his precious stick at her feet once more and looked pleadingly up at her from liquid brown eyes.

'What a good, clever boy you are,' she said indulgently, and threw the stick again.

This game continued for the next half an hour, by which time Olivia was ready to return to the house. She led Brutus to the kitchen door, surprising her servants by entering that way with the hound following behind her.

'I'll put that brute out,' the kitchen wench said and prepared to do so, but Olivia stopped her.

'No, let him come in,' Olivia said. 'I wondered if Cook would give him a bone?'

'Yes, of course, milady,' Cook said, bustling up to her. 'I was wishful to know if you wanted to make a change to the menus, milady?'

'Not for the moment,' Olivia said. 'The roast you served last night was delicious and so were the sweetbreads in cream sauce. My lord particularly enjoyed those—and the trifle was delicious. Why do you not continue with your menus as usual for a week or two? Then I can decide what changes we would like to make, if any.'

'Yes, milady.' Cook said and smiled. She glanced at the dog. 'I've not seen that brute so friendly with anyone except the master. Will a ham bone do for him?'

'Yes, I think that should do very nicely,' Olivia said. 'He may take it outside so he will not be in your way.'

She watched as Cook fetched the bone from the larder and showed it to the dog. He looked at it with anticipation, following her to the door, but then when Olivia did not accompany her, he stood obstinately, whining, his head turned towards her.

'Well, I never,' Cook said. 'It seems he would rather be with you than have the bone, milady.'

'Yes, so it does,' Olivia said and laughed, surprised and pleased by this show of devotion. 'Well, if one of the footmen were to bring a blanket to my parlour, I dare say he would not make so very much mess.'

'You'll not bring that brute inside the house?' Cook looked astounded.

'He is not such a brute,' Olivia said. 'I know he is a little ugly, but I like him. I think that if his manners are respectable we might allow him inside, don't you?'

Cook was clearly doubtful, but Olivia was mistress and there was no gainsaying her. 'I'll ask Henry to bring an old blanket in to you at once, milady.'

'Don't forget the bone,' Olivia said. 'We shall not make a habit of it. Brutus will take his meals here or outside, but just this once I think he may be indulged.'

'Just as you wish,' Cook said, shaking her head as Olivia went out, followed by her shadow. 'Well, I never. That brute allowed in the house. Sir Joshua would turn in his grave.'

Olivia returned to her parlour and sat down in a high-backed wing chair near the fireplace. Brutus lay down at her feet, his head on his front paws, eyes watching her. Even when the footman came in a few minutes later, he did not move until she stood up and walked over to the blanket.

'That is for you,' she said. 'For being a good dog. Do you not want it? Lie down and eat your bone, there's a good boy.' She walked back to the fireplace and sat down; Brutus followed, squatting at her feet. 'Oh, you foolish creature,' Olivia cried. 'Why do you not eat it?'

'Because he knows it is not allowed,' said a voice from the doorway. 'Are you intending to make him your lapdog, Olivia? He has been reared to the outdoors, to protect this estate and its people.'

'Ah, there you are, my lord,' Olivia said. 'They told me you had gone riding earlier. Did you enjoy the outing?'

'I had business with one of my tenants,' Jack said, and sat down in the chair opposite her. 'Forgive me for deserting you. I trust you were not bored?'

'How could I be bored?' Olivia asked, smiling at him. 'I have been looking over the house. I told you Mrs Jenkins was to take me round—do you not remember? And then, I went outside and Brutus found me.'

'You told me you were terrified of dogs,' Jack said, his brows raised. 'You appear to have conquered your fear, Olivia.'

'I saw that I had no choice,' she said. 'Brutus was watching me suspiciously. Had I shown I was nervous I should always have been at a disadvantage with him, you see. Now we are friends and I have no need to feel nervous if I come upon him in the grounds.'

'From what I can see of things, he has become your shadow, Olivia,' Jack remarked with a wry twist of his lips. 'I beg you not to spoil him too much or he will become useless as a guard dog.'

'I dare say you could buy another one,' Olivia said, a dimple in her cheeks. 'I have taken a fancy to him, Jack—may I not have him for my own?'

'Minx!' he murmured, eyes bright with amusement. 'I dare say you will do as you please, whether I give my permission or not.'

'Oh, no,' she said on a gurgle of laughter. 'I mean to be a good and obedient wife to you, Jack. I shall do whatever you tell me.'

'Indeed?' He looked his disbelief. 'I take leave to doubt that, madam wife. I think you will twist the servants round your little finger just as you have this foolish beast. I have no doubt you have most of them eating out of your hand already.'

'I think it is always best to respect the people who work for you, and to have them respect you—do you not agree, my lord?'

'I dare say,' he said, a reluctant smile on his lips. 'So, my lady, what shall we do this afternoon? Would you like to go for a carriage drive—or would you prefer to ride?'

'Have you a horse in your stable that would suit me?' Olivia asked. She smiled as he nodded. 'Then I should like to go riding with you—if you could bear it?'

'It is one of the pastimes we could share,' Jack said. 'I shall be pleased to show you the estate, Olivia.'

'Then I shall change after nuncheon,' she said. 'I believe there is a cold collation being prepared for us in the breakfast parlour—if you are hungry, my lord?'

'I dare say I could eat a few morsels,' he said, a gleam in his eyes. 'And if you continue to my lord me, Olivia, I shall take a stick to you! A husband is allowed to beat his wife, you know.'

Olivia laughed, her eyes bright with challenge. 'A husband is allowed many privileges, Jack. For myself I would deny you none of them.'

Jack came to her and took her hand, turning it over to kiss the palm. 'For now I shall not avail myself of your generosity,' he said. 'But perhaps one day…'

'That day cannot come too soon for me,' Olivia said. 'But I find I am hungry. Pray let us eat…'

Olivia's heart was racing. Jack's black mood seemed to have gone. He was almost the man who had courted her at Camberwell, the man who had flirted with her in Brighton. He had clearly decided that if they were to live together at all, he must offer her companionship.

At least that was a start, Olivia thought. If they could be friends and companions, surely in time they could also be lovers?

She could not guess at the hours Jack had spent

wrestling with his conscience, or that this softer mood, which had descended on him for the moment, came from his decision to write to the Earl of Heggan.

Jack knew that he must discover the truth of his father's madness or he would never find true peace. He must know whether Viscount Stanhope's insanity was hereditary or due to some disease that had come upon him. His love for Olivia was such that he had come to a difficult and painful decision during the long hours of the night. If indeed the madness was in his blood, he must release Olivia from this marriage. It would not be fair to her to continue this sham for the rest of their lives. He must let her go, as hard as that might be for both of them.

Yet for a while he would savour her presence in his home. He would offer her friendship and kindness if he could give her no more—and if part they must, he would have her understand why he was sending her away.

Unaware of Jack's thoughts, Olivia had begun insensibly to hope. His smiles made her heart beat a wild tattoo, and his nearness made her faint with longing. She smiled up at him, her lips parting in invitation of a kiss, and did not know how she tempted him, how it tore him apart to turn away from her teasing looks.

And so they sat down to eat nuncheon together on their first day in their new home, and the huge dog that had unknowingly brought them together lay in the doorway and watched over them.

Chapter Nine

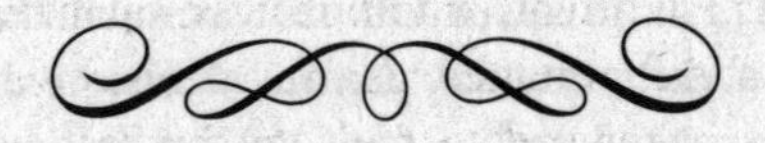

Jack knew that she had been in his room again; he could sense her presence, smell the perfume that seemed to trail behind her wherever she went. She was mistress of the house. He could not deny her access to his rooms. She came and went as she pleased, as was her right.

He smiled as he saw the rose and the note on his pillow. She had left something for him every night of the three weeks they had been married, and he had come to expect it, to anticipate it, if the truth were told, with an eagerness he would not admit even to himself.

He had discovered that the key to the dressing-room had disappeared from his side of the door on their second night at Briarwood. It had been placed on the chest of drawers in the room, which divided them, with a note asking if he was perhaps afraid she wandered in her sleep and might disturb him. She had promised faithfully not to do so and wished him sweet dreams. Jack had left the key where it lay. If this was to be a battle of wills then so be it. Yet it was becoming harder and harder not to go through that door and claim his bride.

He smiled as he scanned her latest note and then placed it with the others between the covers of a poetry book she had recommended to him. Olivia was enchanting, a bright, intelligent companion, always ready to share his interests, never fussy or petulant, her smiles calculated to melt the hardest heart—and Jack's heart had long ago been won.

He had hoped to have a reply from the Earl of Heggan before this, but there was still no word. God, how much he wanted to take Olivia in his arms, to kiss her and make love to her! His flesh felt as if it were on fire, and he knew that once again he would lie without sleeping for most of the night, until at last he was driven to leave the house.

Brutus joined him on his nightly walks, but the dog had given its true allegiance to Olivia, and was a constant reminder that she had bewitched them all.

Perhaps if they were to have guests...yes, that might help. They were spending too much time in each other's company. He would suggest they give a dinner for their neighbours, who must be waiting for some sort of sign that visitors would be welcome. Jack nodded to himself. Yes, that would make things easier. He would suggest it to Olivia in the morning.

Olivia was in the parlour reading a letter when Jack entered that morning. He was dressed in russet coat and fawn breeches, his neckcloth tied in a plain knot, and had clearly been out riding. The sight of him made her heart leap as always, and she smiled up at him, showing him what she held in her hand.

'Beatrice sent this on to me,' she said. 'It is from Lady Burton. She apologises for not having come to our wedding. Apparently she was unwell and was not given my invitation until it was too late for a reply.'

Jack frowned. 'Do you believe that to be true, Olivia?'

'I do not know,' she admitted. 'I think she may have been afraid of disobeying her husband—for it was he who forbade her to see me.'

'But now she has written to you?'

'She asks if she may come to visit me, and begs me to forgive her for her unkindness...'

'Do you wish to see her?'

Olivia looked thoughtful for a moment, then inclined her head. 'Yes, I think perhaps I do, Jack. She was a gentle, kind mother to me when I was growing up. A little over-protective perhaps, and nervous—but I believe she did care for me.'

'And you care for her, despite what she did to you?'

'Lord Burton gave her no choice.'

'Then you must write and invite her to come,' Jack said. 'I was about to ask you if you would like to give a dinner for our neighbours. I think that perhaps it is time we began to see our friends. Do you not agree?'

'I see no reason why we should not,' Olivia replied. 'What shall we do today? Shall we ride—or will you walk with me in the gardens? There is some planting I have in mind near that pretty temple at the edge of the wood. Would you like to discuss it, or shall I speak to the gardeners alone?'

Every day these past weeks she had had some scheme to keep him bound to her side. Jack was well aware that he was losing this battle between them, that his will was growing weaker by the hour.

'I have some business to attend,' he said. 'You will have to excuse me, Olivia. Please do as you think fit. You have no need to consult me if you wish to make changes.'

'Very well, I shall speak to the gardeners this afternoon. And I shall write to Lady Burton this morning. If you are sure you do not mind?'

'You may invite anyone you please,' Jack replied with a frown. 'This is your home, Olivia.'

'Yes, of course,' she said, and for a moment the sadness in her eyes almost tore the heart from his breast, but then before he could speak or move she was smiling again. 'You must give me a list of your friends, Jack. People you want to invite to dine or to stay.'

'You will find one in the desk in my study,' he replied. 'Choose as you will, it matters little to me.'

'Very well,' she said and stood up. She came up to him, laying her hand on his arm. 'I am sure I shall like all your friends, dearest Jack. I think I shall invite a few guests for when Lady Burton comes to stay; it will be more comfortable that way.'

'As you please,' Jack muttered, and turned away lest she see how her touch affected him. 'Excuse me now, I have things to do.'

Olivia watched as he turned and strode from the room, her smile fading. It was so hard not to give way to despair sometimes, but she was determined not to give up. She would not let go. She would hold on until Jack was ready to tell her why he was keeping this distance between them, even though it was hurting them both so much.

'Yes, milady.' The gardener touched his forehead respectfully. 'I agree with you, it would be better if that area by the temple was cleared and laid out with lawns and small bushes. Those old trees have grown too tall and cast a heavy shade.'

'Then you will see to it?' Olivia asked. 'I should like to be able to use the temple in autumn as well as in summer.'

She smiled and nodded then walked away, calling to Brutus to follow. It was a warm afternoon and she felt like walking further than she had previously, so she made no attempt to restrain the dog when he bounded into the woods ahead of her.

It was pleasant in the woods, the sunlight filtering through the canopy of leaves overhead. Olivia thought about the woods near her father's home in Abbot Giles. She had not liked to walk there because of the

Marquis of Sywell, but she had often wondered about the Sacred Grove that was said to lie deep in its heart. She wondered if there was a sacred grove here, and whispered a secret prayer to the Lady of the Woods.

'Make him come to me,' she whispered. 'Please, let him love me.'

Olivia wandered for half an hour or more, lost in her thoughts.

Just why was Jack still holding back from her? She had seen him looking at her sometimes when he thought she was not aware of it, and she had sensed that he was holding himself on a tight rein. Surely she was not wrong in thinking that he loved her? She could not be mistaken! She was certain he was as unhappy about their unnatural situation as she was.

'Who 'ave we 'ere, my pretty?' a rough voice said from behind her. Startled, Olivia spun round to find herself face to face with a man who had stepped out from the trees, a man who by his garb and looks must be one of the gypsies Jack had once warned her about in these very woods. 'I reckon as you'll be 'is lordship's missus…and a right pretty piece you be, an' all.'

Olivia swallowed hard, standing absolutely still as the man came nearer. She did not care for the way he was staring at her. She glanced over her shoulder, looking for Brutus, but she knew he was running on ahead of her.

'What are you doing here?' Olivia found her voice at last. 'You should not be on my husband's land.'

'Not good enough for the likes of you, that's what I reckon you and your 'usband think,' he muttered, eyes narrowed. 'Well, he ain't here now, is he? So I reckon as I'll just sample his wares…'

'Do not dare to touch me,' Olivia said, taking a step back. She ought never to have come here alone! Jack had warned her of it that very first day. 'If you lay a finger on me, my husband will see that you are punished for it.'

'I reckon as I'll take me chances on that…' The man licked his lips as if in anticipation of a treat.

'No!' Olivia turned and began to run. She was terrified of the brute pursuing her. Somehow she must get away from him! She screamed out for help as she heard the crash of his feet behind her. He was gaining on her. He would catch her very soon. The thought filled her with horror. She gave a terrified cry and stumbled, then felt a lurching sensation as he threw himself at her and she was knocked to the ground. 'Help me!' She screamed wildly. 'Brutus! Oh, please help me…'

The man was tearing at her clothes, forcing her skirts up to her thighs, his filthy hands pawing at her flesh. The stench of him was in her nostrils, making her want to retch as she struggled beneath the weight of his body.

'Brutus! Help me…'

Even as the despairing cry left Olivia's lips she heard a terrible growling and felt the impact as the dog landed on top of the man, biting and snarling in a flurry of blood, claws and teeth. For a few moments Olivia was trapped beneath them both as the man turned to fight off his vicious attacker. Then, as they rolled away together, she was suddenly free. She jumped to her feet and sped away into the trees, the sounds of the terrible fight following her, making her put her hands to her ears to shut out the horror.

Olivia did not stop running until she reached the gardens of Briarwood House. There she suddenly bent over double, gasping, her breath coming in huge sobbing breaths.

'Olivia!' She whirled round as she heard Jack's voice, then ran to him, throwing herself into his arms as he opened them to her. 'What has happened? What is it, my darling? You must tell me.'

'He...he attacked me...' She was trembling, crying.

'Brutus? I'll have the brute shot!'

'No!' Olivia cried. 'We were walking in the woods...a gypsy tried to...' She gulped back her tears. 'Brutus saved me. He attacked the gypsy and I ran.' She lifted her eyes to Jack in a desperate appeal. 'You must send men to look for Brutus. I heard him yelp as I ran away. I think the gypsy may have had a knife. Brutus may be hurt.'

'I shall send someone as soon as I have you safe inside the house,' Jack said, and bent down to sweep Olivia up in his arms. 'I'll have the lot of them hanged for this!'

'No, no, you must not blame them all for what one

man did,' Olivia begged. Her lovely eyes were filled with tears as she suddenly realised what had almost happened to her. She hid her face against his shoulder, bravely holding back her desire to weep.

'They shall not dare to come here again,' Jack said, his mouth hard, eyes angry. Once before he had been too late to help a woman in distress, prevented by illness and orders from his commander from seeking out the offenders and administering punishment. This time he would not fail! 'The one who attacked you must be made an example of—and the rest taught a lesson they will not forget.'

Olivia made a murmur of protest against his shoulder. For once in her life she did not feel capable of arguing.

Mrs Jenkins came out into the hall as Jack carried her in, the housekeeper's cries of alarm bringing Jenkins and other servants to see what had happened.

'Lady Stanhope has been attacked in the woods by a gypsy,' Jack said, giving Jenkins a significant look. 'And Brutus may have been wounded. Send to the stables. I want every available man out in those woods. The dog is to be found and that wretch...'

'Yes, milord,' Jenkins said. He glanced warningly in Olivia's direction. 'The men will know what to do.'

Jack nodded. He carried Olivia up the stairs, one of the maids running on ahead to open the door of her bedchamber. The girl pulled back the covers so that he could deposit his wife gently against the pillows. He frowned as he noticed the mud and debris clinging to her gown and the cuts on her arms and cheek.

'There is blood,' he said, touching her face. 'You were hurt, my love.'

The concern in his eyes brought the tears spilling over. 'It is nothing,' Olivia said through her tears. 'I may have been scratched a little in the struggle, but Brutus was in time to—to save me from worse.'

'Thank God for that!' Jack said, a grimace on his lips. 'In future he can take his bone wherever he wishes. He shall never be far from your side, Olivia.'

'If only he is not hurt,' she said with a sob in her voice, though the tears had ceased.

'You leave her ladyship with me now, sir,' Mrs Jenkins offered. 'I'm sure all our minds would be set at rest to know that dog is safe—for the creature has been a hero this afternoon and no mistake.'

'Yes.' Jack looked at Olivia. 'It is best I leave you now, my love. Mrs Jenkins will take care of you. I think that perhaps we should ask the doctor to call…'

'Yes, milord. I'll send someone straight away,' Mrs Jenkins said, but a plea from Olivia stopped her from ringing for the maid.

'No, please, it is not necessary,' Olivia said. 'It was just the shock, but I am better now. If I lie here quietly for half an hour I shall soon recover.'

'We'll see how her ladyship feels in a little while,' the housekeeper said. 'I think what madam needs now is a nice wash and a soothing tisane.'

'Yes, that is just what I need,' Olivia agreed. 'Will

you have hot water sent up please, Mrs Jenkins? And if you would be so kind as to leave me alone—both of you?' Olivia lay back and closed her eyes.

'I shall come to see you when I have discovered what has happened to your dog,' Jack said in a choked voice and went out.

'The tisane will help you to sleep, milady.'

Olivia sighed as the door closed behind them both. She turned her face to the pillow, letting herself weep for a few minutes. Then she sat up in bed and wiped her eyes with the sleeve of her gown. This was so foolish! She had nothing to show for her fright but a few cuts and bruises. Weeping over it would do no one any good!

She left the bed and went behind the painted screen to take off her clothes. A moment or two later, she heard the maid returning with her can of hot water and waited until she had departed. Sure that she was alone, Olivia went over to her washstand and poured the water into a pretty porcelain basin. She washed herself from head to toe, rubbing the scented soap into her skin until she could no longer even imagine she could still smell the stink of that man on her flesh. She was fully dressed in a clean muslin gown when the housekeeper returned with the tisane.

'Will you not lie down for a while?' Mrs Jenkins asked, looking concerned. 'It must have been a terrible shock for you, milady.'

'It was a little frightening,' Olivia admitted. 'But I

am over it now, thank you.' She looked at Mrs Jenkins anxiously. 'Is there any news of poor Brutus?'

'Not yet, milady,' replied the housekeeper. 'Is there anything more I can do for you?'

'You have already been very kind,' Olivia said. 'I think I shall take your advice and lie down for a few moments.' She took the glass of hot, spicy liquid from Mrs Jenkins and sipped it cautiously. 'Oh, this is pleasant.'

'You drink it all up,' the housekeeper advised. 'Rest for an hour or so, madam. I am sure you will be the better for it.'

Olivia was anxious about her dog, but decided she would put her feet up on the daybed and rest for a little while. She had meant to go downstairs as soon as she was dressed, but there was really no point. Jack had promised to tell her as soon as he had news.

She carried the glass to her comfortable daybed and sat down; continuing now and then to sip the drink Mrs Jenkins had prepared for her, she finished every drop. Setting the glass down on the table beside her, she reached for the book of poems lying there. However, her eyelids felt heavy and she lay back, closing them as the odd lethargy claimed her. Perhaps it would do no harm to sleep for a moment or two.

Jack paused on the threshold as he saw Olivia sleeping. She looked so lovely, so vulnerable—and he might have lost her! Had Brutus not been there when she needed help, she would undoubtedly have been raped and would perhaps be dead or dying even now.

He could not bear to lose her! God, forgive him but he loved her too much to give her up. She was more precious to him than his own life. Without her he would have no reason for living.

She stirred as he moved towards her, and then her eyes opened and she smiled. 'Jack,' she said, holding out her arms to him. 'I was dreaming of you and you have come to me.'

'Olivia,' he murmured huskily. 'Olivia—I adore you. You are so lovely, so far above me…'

'Why so, my lord?' she asked, her eyes glowing as she gazed up at him. She stood up, moving towards him, her lips soft with invitation. 'I am only a woman, a woman who loves her husband and would be a true wife to him.'

'Olivia…' Jack's voice broke. He could not move or speak. His resistance seemed to have melted like snow in the sun, and he forgot all the promises he had made to himself to keep a distance between them. 'My lovely, lovely woman.'

In another moment she was in his arms. He gazed down at her as a man dying of thirst might gaze at a spring of cool water, and then his mouth came down to take possession of hers. The kiss seemed to go on and on, their hunger for each other overtaking all other considerations. With a groan of resignation, Jack swept her up and carried her into the bedroom, laying her down on the bed, resting one knee upon it to gaze down at her.

'I cannot hold back any longer,' he muttered hoarsely. 'I am damned for what I do, but I love you too much. Forgive me, Olivia.'

'Do not talk of forgiveness,' she said, her arms going up to stroke his cheek lovingly. 'I want this as much as you, Jack. No matter what causes you such torture, we shall face it together. I love you and I always shall. Believe me, we were meant to be one…'

Jack could not have left her now if he died for it. He bent to kiss her again, flicking at her with his tongue, teasing her, savouring the sweetness of her mouth. She tasted of honey and wine, and he felt as if she intoxicated him, making him forget everything but her sweetness and his need for her.

Somehow they divested themselves of their clothing, gown and breeches abandoned to lie carelessly side by side on the floor. Impatiently, they reached for each other, needing, wanting to be one.

For Olivia, Jack's kisses and caresses were all her dreams come true; she surrendered her whole self to him, giving herself up to the pleasure his loving was revealing to her. This was what she had longed for night after night in her lonely bed; this was her heart's desire.

She arched her back as his kisses traced their way down her navel, quivering with sensual delight as for a moment Jack rested his face against the softness of her feminine hair. He stroked her thighs, his lips kissing and tasting every part of her, even her ankles and her feet.

'My angel,' he murmured. 'I knew you would be thus. I have thought of you every minute of every night that I have lain apart from you. I adore you, Olivia. I shall always cherish and protect you.'

Olivia clung to him, her hands moving over the hard but silken contours of his shoulders. Oh, how she loved this man! How she longed to be his, joined as of one flesh. He had brought her to fever pitch with his lips and his gentle but firm stroking, so that when at last he entered her, her cry was more of pleasure than of pain.

That first slight pain was soon forgotten as their bodies strove to match each other's, meeting in a surge of such delight that Olivia felt as if she were fainting, falling into the pleasure. Jack cried out, and then at last they were both still, holding each other as though they would never be torn apart.

They lay for some time entwined as one, then Olivia turned to her husband who was at last truly hers, and reached up to touch his face with her fingertips.

'And so, my lord,' she whispered. 'We are one now. Will you not tell me why you held back so long?'

'Later,' he said and rolled away from her. As she lay watching, he pulled on his breeches and shirt and gathered up his remaining garments. 'I promise I shall tell you, Olivia—this evening, after dinner.'

'As you wish,' she said, half wishing she had not spoken as she saw the shadows come back to his face. 'You have not told me about Brutus—was he much harmed?'

'He received a knife wound in the shoulder which has bled considerably,' Jack said, frowning. 'It will heal, I think. I have told my head groom to tend him as if he were my best thoroughbred stallion. Have faith, Olivia. We shall do our best for your wretched dog.'

'I know you will,' she said and smiled at him. She did not ask about the gypsy who had attacked her. There were some things it was wiser for a woman not to know. 'I love you, Jack. Do not regret what has happened here, for I shall not.'

'You may change your mind when you know all,' Jack said. 'But it is done now and we may not go back if we would.'

Olivia watched as he went from the room. A chill ran through her, and she wondered what could be so terrible that it had brought such a look to Jack's eyes.

She had only to be patient for a while longer. Olivia hugged the memory of Jack's passionate loving to her as she rose and washed before choosing a gown for the evening. Her maid had not come at the usual time, but perhaps she had guessed that Lord and Lady Stanhope were together? Olivia blushed as she realised this must be so. The servants always knew everything!

She stood in her shift and rang the bell for Rosie.

She could not manage to fasten her evening-gown alone, and she needed help to dress her hair. She tried not to blush, avoiding the girl's knowing look as she came in answer to the summons.

'I waited for you to ring, milady,' Rosie said. 'I hope I did right?'

'Yes, quite right,' Olivia replied with dignity. 'My lord was with me—we had something to discuss.'

'Yes, milady.'

Olivia saw the girl's smirk. No doubt it would soon be common knowledge below stairs that my Lord and Lady Stanhope had been making love before dinner!

'I have decided I shall wear my hair loose this evening,' Olivia said as Rosie finished fastening her gown at the back. 'You may go now, thank you.'

'Yes, milady.' Rosie bobbed a curtsey as the door to the dressing-room opened and Jack entered. 'Thank you, milady.' She ran away giggling after throwing a sly look at her master.

'I suppose she was listening at the keyhole,' Jack said, lips twisting wryly. 'You would not be able to seek an annulment now, Olivia.'

'What matter, since I do not wish for it?'

'I brought you this,' Jack said, presenting her with velvet box. 'It was meant as a trinket for our wedding night…'

Olivia took the box and opened it, giving a cry of pleasure as she saw the diamond necklace inside. She turned and kissed him on the cheek, trying not to notice as he half flinched away from her touch.

'Thank you, Jack,' she said and smiled. 'Will you fasten them for me, please?'

'Yes, of course.'

He took the necklace and placed it about her throat, giving her an odd half smile. 'Diamonds become you very well, my lady.'

'Yes, I think so,' Olivia said and touched the pendant, which was shaped like a heart. 'The stones are very fine, Jack. I shall have occasion to wear them when our guests visit next weekend.'

'You sent the invitations then?'

'Yes,' she replied. 'Of course not everyone may be able to come. But I think we can count on Lady Burton—and I invited your friend Viscount Gransden. Lord and Lady Melford as well. They live only a few miles away, but too far to come simply for dinner so I asked them to stay for the weekend. Sir Ralph Peterson and his daughter Sarah, whom I knew in London, are at home in the country and but two miles from us. I have however offered them the chance to stay the weekend if they so wish.'

'As I said earlier, you are mistress here. You must do just as you wish, Olivia.'

Jack was being meticulously polite, but she sensed he was holding back from her once more. It seemed to Olivia that his manner was subdued, that he was not quite able to meet her eyes. Why? She sensed that he was feeling a sense of shame. Surely not! Why should he? There was no shame in consummating their marriage, especially when they were so much in love.

'Shall we go down, dearest?' she asked, slipping her arm through his and smiling up at him. 'We do not want to keep Cook waiting—or goodness knows what they will be imagining below stairs.'

'They will say that I am so besotted by my wife that I would prefer to make love to her than eat dinner,' Jack smiled and for a moment the shadows had gone. 'In thinking that, they would be right, Olivia. However, it is not good manners to keep one's servants waiting.'

Olivia laughed as she saw the expression in his eyes. Whatever Jack was keeping from her, he could no longer even attempt to hide his feelings for her. She squeezed his arm as they went out into the hall. Surely it could not be so very bad? Whatever had been hurting Jack all this time, they could face it together.

'I shall not blame you if you hate me,' Jack said as he brought his story to an end. 'Had the circumstance of our engagement been other than it was, I should naturally have asked you to release me from my promise to marry you. However, I felt that you might gain more from the kind of marriage I was still able to offer...but I was wrong. I should have told you the truth and let you decide for yourself.'

Olivia was gripping her hands in her lap so tightly that her nails cut into the palms. Surely this was a nightmare from which she would eventually awake? Jack's father a raving lunatic at his death...the possibility that the sickness was hereditary? It could not be true. It was too terrible! Too horrible to contemplate.

Yet she knew that Jack had spoken every word from his heart. It had hurt him to speak the truth, a truth that so clearly explained the reasons for his reluctance to come to her bed.

She swallowed hard, her throat dry and painful. 'If we have a child...' Her eyes were dark with horror as she gazed up at him, knowing that she might already be carrying his seed in her womb. 'It would be all right...wouldn't it, Jack?'

'I cannot lie to you,' Jack said hoarsely. 'It has been my fear that this dread sickness may be carried in my blood. I have written to the Earl of Heggan asking him to tell me what he knows, but he has not yet replied.'

'And if...' She moistened her lips with the tip of her tongue.

'If it is true, there must never be a child,' Jack said harshly. His face was grey with anguish. 'What happened this afternoon was wrong, Olivia.'

'How can you say that?' she cried, leaping to her feet and moving towards him. 'What you have told me makes no difference to our love. I am still your wife, Jack. I love you...'

'And I love you,' he said, but stepped back from her, his eyes still intent on her face. 'But you must understand that if…if you can bear me near you knowing this…we must never give way to our feelings in the same way. We must be vigilant. You can never bear my child, Olivia.'

'Never have your child…' Olivia stifled a sob, but not before he had heard it and seen the grief his words had caused her.

'Forgive me,' he said. 'I should never have married you. Perhaps it is not too late…an annulment is out of the question, of course. I will give you cause for divorce. There will be scandal, but you could go abroad, Olivia. My fortune is at your…'

She moved towards him swiftly, pressing her fingers to his mouth to stop the words, which were breaking her heart. 'Do not say it,' she cried. 'I beg you not to consider divorce. I do not wish to leave you, nor shall I marry again. No other man could ever take your place in my heart.'

'Then I have ruined your life,' Jack said. 'I wish I could turn back the clock, my darling, but it is too late.'

'Do not withdraw from me,' Olivia begged. 'This is a cruel blow for us both, but we must struggle to accept it. Perhaps the Earl will write soon and all your fears will have been for nothing.'

'I would give a fortune if that were so,' Jack said. 'I have been weak and now my selfishness has destroyed you—the woman I love more than life itself.'

'Hush, my love,' Olivia said softly. 'You speak foolishly. You have not destroyed me—or damaged my love for you. I own that it will grieve me if we can never have a child, but if that is the price we must pay to be together, I shall pay it and gladly.'

'You would not turn from me?' Jack asked. 'I have been afraid to see horror and disgust in your eyes, Olivia. Can you truly say that this has not changed your feelings even a little?'

Olivia gazed up at him. It would be a lie to say her feelings had not changed; she thought they had become stronger, perhaps more mature.

'Jack, I…' she paused, not knowing quite how to say what was in her heart. It was a brief moment of hesitation but it was too much for Jack. He flinched as though she had struck him, then turned and strode away from her. 'Jack! Jack, come back. I have not changed. I love you as much and more.'

He turned to look at her from the doorway. 'You are brave, Olivia,' he said. 'I know that well, but I can see the doubts in your eyes. I beg your pardon for my weakness this afternoon. If I can find a way to make reparation, I shall.'

'Please do not leave me,' she cried. 'Please do not go, Jack.'

Tears gathered in her eyes as the door closed behind him. Why had she hesitated even for that brief second of time? She loved him, needed him—did not believe for one moment that he himself was afflicted with his father's madness.

Yet, there was a small voice inside her that asked what might happen in the years to come. Jack had seen that in her eyes even though she was not truly aware of the thought.

How that must have hurt him! Olivia wished that she had been able to give him the reassurance that he needed so badly. She did love him; she loved him so much that she did not know what she would do with her life if Jack left her. Yet she had felt a moment of fear for the unknown future.

'Please do not go,' she whispered to the empty room. 'Please do not leave me, my darling Jack. If you do, I would rather die than live without you.'

Chapter Ten

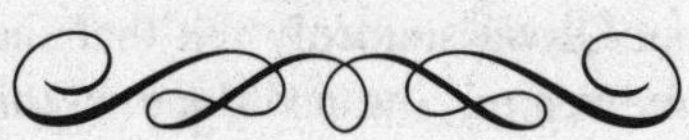

Olivia's guests had begun to arrive. She had already welcomed Lord and Lady Melford, and they were being shown up to their bedchamber. She was this very moment at her desk in the little parlour, glancing through a letter she had just received from Beatrice. It appeared that there was some interesting news from Abbot Giles concerning the Earl of Yardley and Steepwood Abbey…but she could hear voices in the hall. More guests were arriving. She put the letter aside for later and rose to her feet, smiling a greeting as Viscount Gransden and Lady Burton were shown into the room one after the other.

'Lady Stanhope…' Leander Gransden came forward to take the hand she proffered. He raised it to his lips gallantly. 'It is delightful to meet you again.'

'I am pleased to welcome you to Briarwood.' She glanced at Lady Burton, who was still standing uncertainly just inside the door. 'I am not sure whether you know my aunt, sir? Lady Burton—Lord Gransden.'

'I believe we may have met on a previous occasion,' the Viscount said, glancing at Lady Burton. He bowed over her hand but did not kiss it. 'But I am happy to renew our acquaintance, ma'am.'

His manners were perfect, his smile devastatingly charming, but Olivia suddenly felt that she had been unwise to invite him. She had done so thinking him one of Jack's closest friends, but there was something in the way he had kissed her hand that made her a little wary of him. At her wedding he had seemed very pleasant, but now she thought he might be a rake. She had met others of his ilk and learned to be wary of them.

'I shall have Jenkins take you up, Lord Gransden,' she said. 'I must apologise for Jack. He was to…ah, here he is at last,' she said, and smiled at her husband. 'I had almost given you up, my lord.'

'Forgive me, I was delayed. Gransden, my apologies.' Jack smiled at Lady Burton. 'You will excuse us, ma'am? We shall have the opportunity to talk later. For now I am sure you would like to be private with Olivia.'

'You are very kind, sir.'

Jack turned back to the Viscount. 'Come to the library and take a glass of Madeira with me, Gransden.'

'Willingly,' the Viscount replied.

Olivia's gaze met that of Lady Burton as the men

went out together. She hesitated for a moment; then, sensing the older woman's awkwardness, went forward to kiss her on the cheek.

'You are very welcome here, Aunt.'

The faded blue eyes were moist with tears. 'You used to call me Mama, Olivia.'

Lady Burton was a small woman. She seemed more fragile than Olivia had remembered her, her face thin and pale, her expression permanently anxious.

'But you are in truth my aunt,' Olivia reminded her gently. 'I do not speak of you as such to hurt you, ma'am. I know that the breach between us was not of your making.'

'I have so much regretted it,' Lady Burton said, dabbing at her eyes with a lace kerchief. 'I never ceased to love you, Olivia, despite what you must have thought. Can you ever forgive me for allowing Burton to cast you out?'

'You were not to blame,' Olivia said. 'I think of you kindly, Aunt, and I bear you no ill will. Indeed, it would please me if we could be friends.'

Lady Burton blew her nose hard. Olivia had changed so much. She had been an innocent girl when she jilted Ravensden, little more than a child, but she was a woman now. A woman of some character who knew her own mind. There was no going back, but perhaps they could move on to a new relationship?

'Yes, I should like to be your friend, Olivia,' she said and smiled a little tremulously.

'What will Lord Burton say?'

'I care not,' her aunt replied defiantly. 'I told him I intended to visit you and he said I could go to the devil for all he cared. Our marriage is over, Olivia. He goes his way and I go mine. I should have had the courage to leave his house long ago.'

'Well, you have done so now, and I am glad for your sake.' Olivia reached for her hand and held it. 'Come, let me take you up to your chamber. We may talk privately for a few minutes before joining my other guests for tea.'

Olivia glanced at her own reflection in the mirror. She was wearing a simple evening gown of jonquil silk; the sleeves were puffed and tied with white ribbons. Around her slender neck she wore the pearls Jack had given her as an engagement present.

A sigh issued from her lips as she thought about her husband. Jack had not ridden away that night, as she had feared he might, but the next morning his manner had reverted back to that of a polite stranger. He was considerate, thoughtful and willing to oblige her in every way, except the one she so desperately craved.

He had not kissed her once this past week. If she tried to show him affection, he drew back from her touch as if he had been stung.

Olivia had tried to apologise for her slight hesitation several times, but he merely smiled his cool smile and shook his head.

'It is I who should beg your pardon,' he replied. 'I

do not reproach you for your doubts, Olivia. Many women would shrink from my touch.'

'You are not insane,' she cried. 'I have never thought it, Jack, even for a moment. Whatever the cause of your father's sickness, it has passed you by.'

'Perhaps…' His eyes had taken on that closed, shuttered expression. 'But for how long? How can we be certain this curse will not descend on me in time?'

'How can anyone know the future for certain?' she argued. 'Do not torture yourself so, my love. Let us take what happiness we may together. I know we may never have a child, but I am willing to accept that without regret.'

Jack had walked away before she finished speaking. She had not wept, for she understood that his grief was even harder to bear than her own. Believing that he had harmed her, he carried guilt and shame as well as despair. It was not so, not so! His loving had brought her nothing but pleasure. Only his stubborn refusal to accept her love for what it was had caused her grief.

Sighing again, she thrust the painful thoughts from her. She had guests waiting, and must not let anyone guess that she was desperately unhappy. Jack was playing his part as the attentive host, and she was obliged to do the same.

Picking up her fan, Olivia went out, along the landing and down the stairs. As the hostess, she must be the first down, ready to greet her guests when they entered the drawing-room.

It was still only a few minutes past six and they were not to dine until a quarter to seven. So Olivia was a little surprised to discover Viscount Gransden before her. He was standing by the window, gazing out at the gardens, but turned at once as she entered.

'Ah, Lady Stanhope,' he murmured and she sensed that he had come early in order to have a few moments alone with her. His gaze went over her with undisguised approval. 'How lovely you look this evening. Yes, quite beautiful. Stanhope is a lucky fellow.'

'You are very kind, sir.'

'Do not look as though you did not believe a word,' Gransden said and raised his brows at her. His manner was teasing, flirtatious, but there was a look in his eyes that disturbed her. She recognized it immediately for what it was—the look of a hunter! 'You must know that you are a very beautiful woman.'

'Beauty is not so very important,' Olivia replied. 'Do you not consider character of more lasting value, my lord?'

'But you have character,' he said silkily. 'I would never deny it. Surely you know that I admire you greatly? Few women would have had the courage—or the inclination!—to jilt Ravensden. Most would have taken him for his fortune and consequence. It takes a certain kind of woman to risk all for love.'

Olivia blushed. He was staring at her so intently, making her feel very warm and uncomfortable.

'Some would say I was rather foolish than brave.'

'Perhaps.' He nodded as if agreeing. 'But you have come about. You are Lady Stanhope—and a happy bride, are you not?'

'Very happy,' Olivia said. She raised her head, meeting his gaze with a challenge. 'We are very much in love.'

'Of course—as all brides and grooms should be,' he said, then glanced at his fingernails. 'Unfortunately, the first bloom of love seldom survives the honeymoon.'

Olivia turned away as Jack entered the room. She smiled brilliantly and went to greet him with a kiss on the cheek. He stiffened slightly but realising they were not alone, did not draw back as he was wont to do when she touched him.

'Lord Gransden was just complimenting me on my looks,' Olivia informed him in a teasing, rallying tone. 'I have told him it is because I am happy and because we are both very much in love, but he says romantic love seldom lasts longer than the honeymoon. Will you tell him he is wrong in our case, Jack?'

'Very wrong,' he replied without hesitation. 'In my own case I believe I shall love you until the day I die, Olivia.'

'Well done, Jack,' Gransden said and laughed. 'Prettily said. I can see she has you hanging on to her petticoat tails.'

Jack frowned, but before he could reply the other guests came chattering into the drawing-room. He turned away as Jenkins came to serve sherry and wine, but for the remainder of the evening his eyes followed his wife wherever she went. He noticed Gransden took every opportunity to touch her arm, or engage her in private conversation, and his frown grew into a scowl.

Damn the man's impudence! How dare he look at her that way?

Jack felt the anger surge inside him, but his honesty reminded him that Olivia would be better off as Gransden's mistress than as Jack's wife. The Viscount could give her so much that was forbidden Jack, for he had made up his mind that there would be no repeat of that afternoon when he had made love to her. It would be best for Olivia's sake if he were to go away, perhaps travel abroad somewhere. She might weep for him at first, but then she would find consolation in the arms of Gransden or someone like him.

Yet the thought of any other man touching her was like a poison barb in Jack's side, and when his friend suggested a private game of cards later that evening, when the ladies had retired to their chambers, he could barely bring himself to be civil to him.

'You must excuse me,' he said. 'I have some pressing affairs I must attend. Perhaps tomorrow...' and with that he walked away, leaving the Viscount to stare after him in surprise.

It seemed that all was not well after all, Gransden thought smiling to himself. How interesting! He scented a mystery. Well, it might prove amusing to see how far he could press the pretty bride. Lady Stanhope was a passionate little thing, if that mouth of hers was anything to the point. He would find it pleasant to spend a few hours in her bed...

The next two days passed very pleasantly. Olivia had no time to think of her own problems as she attended to the comfort of her guests. It was usual for both ladies and gentlemen to keep to their own rooms until almost noon, though Lord Melford and Viscount Gransden were early risers. Since both were keen horsemen, they went riding with their host first thing, then joined the ladies in the breakfast-room for nuncheon.

Olivia too was an early riser these days, and on the Monday morning she met Lord Gransden as she was returning from the garden with a basket of flowers over her arm.

'A very picture of domestic bliss,' the Viscount remarked. 'If I could be certain of securing a bride as...beautiful as you, Lady Stanhope, I might be persuaded into marriage.'

She gave him a reproving look. His manners were easy, his features the kind that would be generally pleasing. Yet she sensed an underlying ruthlessness. 'I am sure there are many pretty young ladies who might be happy to accept a proposal from you, sir.'

'I dare say there are a thousand such,' Gransden replied, moving to block her path as she would have continued on her way towards the house. 'You on the other hand are an exceptional woman, Lady Stanhope.'

'You flatter me, sir.' Olivia tilted her chin at him. This was not the first time this weekend that he had offered her such compliments, and she really did not care for the way he was looking at her. 'You should save your honeyed words for a lady who wishes to hear them. I have no such desire.'

'You are unkind,' Gransden said. He was still smiling but his eyes had narrowed, his wolfish expression sending a chill down her spine. He placed a restraining hand on her arm. 'Stanhope is a dour fellow. You will not wish to spend your life always in the country. When you come to town we might meet in private sometimes.'

'To what end, sir?' Olivia's eyes were angry as she gazed up at him. 'I think we should have little to say to one another.'

'There are more pleasurable ways to spend a dull afternoon,' he said, his finger stroking her bare arm. 'I should be more than happy to find some pastime that might amuse you.'

'I believe I shall decline your offer,' Olivia said. 'And now, if you will excuse me, I must arrange these blooms in water before they start to fade.'

She shook off his hand and walked on determinedly. How dare the Viscount make such suggestions to her? She had been married for a mere four weeks. What could have prompted him to think she might be receptive to his hateful attentions? She could only think that Jack had somehow betrayed the true situation between them.

Surely he would not? It was hurtful to Olivia that her husband might even consider confiding such an intimate secret to his friend. She had not mentioned one word in her letters to Beatrice, nor had she spoken of her unhappiness to Lady Burton. She would not dream of doing so!

She was so angry that she did not notice she was being observed from the windows of the house. It really was too much! No matter how upset Jack was, he should not discuss their situation with another.

She was still feeling angry as she began to arrange her flowers in vases the housekeeper had brought to her private sitting-room. She believed that men did sometimes discuss these things, at least she knew they boasted to one another of their mistresses. She had once hidden behind the curtains in Lord Burton's study and heard some very surprising things. At the time she had been no more than thirteen and too innocent to really understand, but now she knew exactly what they had meant and why they had seemed to think it all so highly amusing!

'Ah, there you are, Olivia,' Jack said entering the room just as she was finishing her flowers. 'The Melfords and Petersons are leaving after nuncheon. I've asked Gransden to stay on until the end of the week. You will want some time to be with Lady Burton when your other guests have gone, and

Gransden knows of some sound carriage horses for sale. We shall ride over later this afternoon to take a look.'

'You must do as you wish.' Olivia frowned. Her heart sank as she contemplated another five days of being leered at by the Viscount. 'It is your house and he is your friend.' Her hurt at his betrayal of her to Gransden made her speak more sharply to him than she ever had before.

'You invited him, Olivia.' Jack's gaze was hard, cold.

She gave him an accusing stare in return. 'Because he was your best friend. Or so I imagined.' A true friend to Jack would not try to make love to her!

'You seem to like him well enough.'

Jack's expression gave nothing away, and Olivia felt her temper rise. How dare he insinuate that she had the slightest interest in the Viscount? Her manner towards him had never been more than that of a hostess concerned for a guest's comfort.

All the frustrations and hurts of the past few weeks boiled over, causing her to speak without thinking.

'Lord Gransden is both charming and handsome, a witty companion. I dare say most women would enjoy his company.' As indeed she would herself if he would not look at her as if he were preparing to gobble her up!

Picking up one of her tastefully arranged rose bowls, she walked past Jack and out into the hall.

Tears were pricking behind her eyes. How could he think so ill of her? What had she done to deserve it?

Olivia placed her bowl on a rather lovely satinwood table in the hall, then ran quickly up the stairs. She heard Jack call her name but would not look back. He had no right to say any such things to her. No right at all!

Olivia and her aunt spent a quiet afternoon together after the other guests had gone. They talked mostly of the past, of the time when Olivia had been Lady Burton's spoiled and much-loved daughter, laughing together easily as they recalled amusing incidents.

'Do you remember that doll you bought me with the wax face and wooden body?' Olivia said. 'I loved poor Betsy so much, but then I threw her in the fish-pond when I was cross and the gardeners had to drain it to get her out.'

'And when they did she was ruined and you wept for hours,' Lady Burton replied, smiling at her fondly. 'I bought you another but it was never the same, was it?'

'No…' Olivia sighed. 'Once something is spoiled it can never be quite the same, can it?'

'No, I suppose not,' Lady Burton said. 'But perhaps in certain cases something better can be put in its place. You were an indulged child, Olivia, and I was a foolish woman, unhappy in my marriage, giving all my love to a child who was not even mine…'

'But you were my mama,' Olivia said. 'I have only good memories of that time.'

'But then Burton disowned you and I let him send you away.'

'That is forgotten now.'

'Then perhaps we can find a true affection for each other as women,' Lady Burton said. 'I would like to believe that when I leave here in a few days you would want to see me again, to visit me—even come to me if you were ever in need of a loving friend.'

'Yes, of course we shall visit one another,' Olivia assured her. 'We shall write often and always be friends.'

'If that is the case, I am content,' her aunt said. She hesitated for a moment, then: 'Forgive me if I intrude into affairs that are none of my business. I do not ask for your confidences, Olivia—but are you quite happy, my dear?'

'Yes, perfectly,' Olivia lied, and then as the other woman's gentle eyes probed. 'I do not like Viscount Gransden very much. Oh, I know he is charming and witty, but he looks at me…in a way that makes me uncomfortable.'

'Yes, I have remarked it,' the older woman said. 'I dare say you will find many men look at you in such a way, my dear. You are beautiful, but there is something more…an indefinable quality that will always draw men to you as moths to a flame.'

'I have noticed that look in some men's eyes before, of course,' Olivia agreed. 'But he seems to imagine I might…it is all nonsense, of course!'

'I saw him waylay you in the garden this morning,' Lady Burton said. 'You must just be firm with him, Olivia, as you were then. Be polite but make sure he understands you are not interested in his attentions. Your husband is a possessive man. I have seen it in his eyes when he looks at you, and of course he adores you.'

'Yes, of course.' Olivia had long since regretted her sharp words that morning. She would take the first opportunity that came her way to apologise to Jack. 'Yes, he does love me, even if he does not always show it.'

'Some men bottle their feelings inside them,' Lady Burton said. 'Do not be upset if your husband does not follow you like a puppy on leading strings. I believe he is a good, kind man. I am happy to see you wed to him, Olivia.'

'Thank you,' she said and got up to go over and kiss Lady Burton's cheek. 'I am so glad you came to stay, Aunt.'

Lady Burton squeezed her hand. 'I loved you when you were a spoiled girl,' she said. 'But I love you even more now that you have become a woman of compassion and generosity.'

'And I love you as a friend and as my dearest aunt,' Olivia said. 'I dare say Jack and Lord Gransden will not be back for hours. I think we should have tea now and not wait for them, do you not agree?'

'There is never any telling when gentlemen will return from a jaunt,' Lady Burton replied with a wry smile. 'Who knows how far they have gone in search of their horses? They may go on somewhere else or stop to dine at an inn before they come home.'

Olivia rang the bell. Lady Burton had made her realise that it was foolish to be angry with Jack over such a little thing, especially as she knew what a strain he was under. She would find a few moments to be alone with him that evening, and try to heal the breach between them.

When the gentlemen did not return by seven, Olivia ordered that dinner be served to her and Lady Burton in the breakfast parlour.

'It is smaller and more cosy for the two of us,' she said to her aunt with a smile. 'We may be comfortable here together.'

After dinner they retired to Olivia's own parlour, where they spent the evening talking. Lady Burton was working on a piece of stitching, which she showed to Olivia on request.

'It is a christening gown,' she said. 'I am making it as a gift for you, my dear.'

'How beautiful,' Olivia said, examining the lace with care. She felt a tearing pain in her heart as she remembered that it would never be worn by Jack's child, but managed to hide her hurt behind a smile. 'You always were clever with your needle. You made such lovely clothes for my poor Betsy.'

At ten o'clock, Lady Burton retired to her bed. 'You will forgive me, Olivia,' she said, 'but I am not used to late hours these days. If I were you I should seek your own bed. When two gentlemen go off together there is no telling but what they may stay out all night.'

'Yes, I think I shall retire soon,' Olivia said. She accompanied Lady Burton to her room, then went along the landing to her own.

It seemed pointless to wait up, yet even after she had allowed Rosie to help her into her night-chemise Olivia was reluctant to seek her bed. She had not expected Jack to stay out so late; he had never done such a thing until now. She wished he had told her they might not be back that evening, and could not help the little nagging voice in her head that whispered he might have been injured.

No, no, she must not allow her imagination to run away with her. Jack was not harmed. He would return to her when he was ready.

It was as she was about to retire to her bed that something alerted her, some slight sound outside—as if someone had knocked against one of the stone vases on the terrace. She crossed over to her window, which was opened a little, and glanced out. In the moonlight she could see two men, and from their behaviour it was clear that one or both were more than a little the worse for strong drink.

'Oh, Jack,' Olivia said, shaking her head as she

turned away to pull on a dressing-robe. 'How could you?'

She was at the head of the stairs when the two men entered the hall. From where she stood, it appeared that Jack was the more intoxicated of the two and was being supported by his friend.

The Viscount glanced up as she began to walk towards them, an odd smile in his eyes. 'Lady Stanhope, I hope you will forgive me for allowing your husband to get into this state. I did warn him, but he would not listen.'

'Not drunk, Olivia,' Jack muttered. 'Just a little bosky. Go to bed.'

'You are the one who needs your bed,' she replied as he seemed to sway on his feet. 'Can you help him upstairs, Lord Gransden? Or shall I summon Jenkins?'

'Library,' Jack said, his voice slightly slurred. 'Sleep it off there, Gransden. Mustn't disturb Olivia.'

'It might be wiser,' the Viscount said apologetically to her. 'Never seen Jack this way. Always carries his drink well.'

Olivia followed behind as Viscount Gransden helped her husband to the library. She watched Jack as he lay back on the sofa and closed his eyes. Was he so desperately unhappy? She had known he stayed on here alone to drink after she had retired for the night, but she had not thought he ended in this state. Why had he taken too much wine this evening?

'Will he be all right there?' she asked. Jack's heavy

breathing seemed to indicate that he had fallen asleep. 'Perhaps I should ask one of the footmen to bring a blanket to cover him.'

'He will do well enough as he is,' Gransden said. She saw the excited glitter in his eyes as they went over her, and was reminded that she was wearing very little clothing. 'By God, you're a beauty! Stanhope is a fool if he does not bed you every night.'

'How dare you!' Olivia cried, incensed. 'You may not speak to me this way, sir. I shall not permit it. Whatever my husband chooses to do is none of your affair. I do not know what he may have said to you, but it makes no difference. I love him and no other!'

'Such passion,' Gransden said, a gleam of appreciation in his eyes. 'Stanhope told me nothing. I never knew such a close-mouthed fellow, even when in his cups. All he would say was that he had let you down.' He moved towards her, suddenly eager. 'If he cannot behave as a husband to you, Olivia, let me show…'

'Come no nearer!' Olivia warned. She reached for the bell-rope and tugged it sharply. 'Be aware, sir! If you attempt to touch me, I shall have my servants throw you out.'

Gransden stared at her in amazement, then to her surprise he began to laugh. 'No, no, madam, I beg you will not go to such lengths to protect your honour. Stanhope's behaviour led me to believe that things were not right between you. I would have seduced you if you were willing—but you have no need to fear me. I have never forced a woman yet, and I have no taste for it.'

'I am glad to hear it, sir,' Olivia replied, relieved that he appeared at last to have accepted her rebuff. 'Whatever is between Jack and me is private. I beg you to respect that and to believe that I love him truly. There will never be another man for me.'

She turned as one of the footmen entered in response to her summons. 'Ah, Thomas. His lordship has been celebrating a little too freely, I fear. Will you look after him for me, please? I should not wish him to come to harm.'

'You may rely on me, milady,' said Thomas, who like the rest of the household had become her devoted follower. 'I shall fetch a blanket to cover him, then stay here all night to watch over his lordship.'

'Thank you,' she said and smiled at him. 'Good night, Lord Gransden. Pray do not trouble yourself to wait up. My husband is in good hands.'

'Good night, Lady Stanhope. Jack is a fortunate man to find such understanding in his wife—and so I shall tell him.'

Olivia nodded and left the room. She was thoughtful as she walked upstairs. It had disturbed her to see her husband intoxicated. If their situation was making Jack so very unhappy perhaps she ought to let him go. It might be better if they lived apart. She would not agree to a divorce, but she could choose to spend much of her time with Lady Burton or her sister.

Chapter Eleven

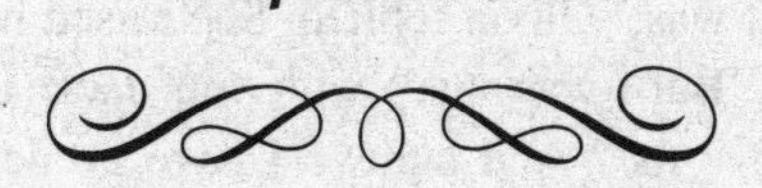

Olivia saw nothing of her husband until late morning the following day. She was once again arranging some roses in a silver bowl when he entered her sitting-room.

Jack stood watching her cut the stems in silence for a moment, then made an odd sound in his throat as he said, 'I must apologise for last evening, Olivia.'

'It does not signify. I worried that you might have met with an accident, but it matters not since you were unharmed. I believe gentlemen do sometimes indulge too freely in their wine.'

'I have never before gone beyond what was acceptable. It was not my intention to do so last evening. I fear I did not notice my glass being refilled…though that does not excuse what happened.'

'Then we shall forget the incident.' Olivia could not bring herself to look at him lest she betray her grief at being the cause of so much pain to him.

'Gransden tells me he intends to leave this afternoon. It seems he has pressing business elsewhere.'

'Then we must not detain him.'

'No…' He hesitated uncertainly. 'I must also beg your pardon for what was said between us yesterday morning. It was unnecessary, untrue and cruel of me.'

'Yes, it was,' Olivia replied. She raised her eyes to meet his. 'But I was sharp with you, Jack. I pray you will forgive me? And believe I have no desire to be in any man's arms but yours?'

'I have always known that in my heart, Olivia. My jealousy made me strike out at you. It is this damnable situation between us!'

'Do you think I do not understand that?' Her eyes were moist with tears she would not shed. 'We both suffer terribly…' He was silent, clearly feeling unable to answer her. Olivia swallowed hard, realising that she must speak if she wanted to save him further pain. 'I think it might be better for us both if I went to stay with Lady Burton until we decide what to do for the best. No one will think it odd if I wish to see her safely home.'

A look of such intense pain crossed Jack's face that she instantly regretted having spoken the words, but it was too late to take them back.

'I do not want a divorce, Jack. Just some time to heal the hurt that is causing us both so much grief.'

Jack inclined his head, his expression wooden. 'Of course. You are very right to suggest it, Olivia. It may be the best for us both,' he said, then turned and strode from the room.

Olivia closed her eyes as the misery swept over her. How could she bear it? Her life was effectively over. She would never be happy again. How could she be when she must forever live apart from the only man she would ever love? Yet she could not bear to see him so desperate, to know that being near her was agony for him.

Olivia raised her head. If they must part, then let the break be made at once. To prolong their agony could only cause unnecessary pain for them both. She loved Jack too much to destroy him. She would give orders for her clothes to be packed and leave in the morning.

'I take my leave of you with regret,' Viscount Gransden said after nuncheon that day. 'You will ask Stanhope to forgive me for not waiting to make my farewells to him?'

'Yes, of course,' Olivia replied. 'He had urgent business with one of his tenants I believe. I know he will be sorry to have missed you.'

Gransden nodded. 'Forgive me if I pressed you too hard. It is a failing with me; I must always go to the edge. I fear I have been used to having my way more than is good for me. Believe me when I say that in future I shall stand your friend. No word of this visit shall leave my lips outside this house. I am sincere when I say that Stanhope is a very fortunate man in his bride.'

'You are gracious, sir—and I shall forgive the slight misunderstanding between us.'

She smiled at him. He was after all a charming man and not the first to try his powers of seduction on her. She offered him her hand. He held it for a moment, then turned and walked from the room. Olivia was about to go in search of her aunt when Mrs Jenkins came in.

'I am sorry to disturb you, milady, but one of the grooms has been here a few minutes ago. He says that Brutus is healing well but…' She pulled a face. 'It seems the poor creature is off his food. It is my opinion that he is pining for you.'

'Oh, my poor Brutus,' Olivia cried, stricken by remorse. 'I have been so concerned with other matters that I have not visited him for two days. I shall go at once.'

Mrs Jenkins smiled her satisfaction. 'I thought you would say that, milady. I took the liberty of sending Rosie for your shawl, and I have packed a basket with tidbits that may tempt the creature's appetite.' She glanced round as the maid knocked and then came in with Olivia's shawl. 'Ah, here is Rosie now.' She took the heavy silk shawl and placed it around Olivia's shoulders. 'The wind is quite cool this afternoon. I believe it may be a foretaste of autumn. We do not want you catching a chill, do we?'

'Thank you for your care of me.' Olivia smiled at her. She would miss Mrs Jenkins when she left here. 'I shall be accompanying Lady Burton to her home tomorrow. Will you have my clothes packed?'

'Will it be a long stay, milady?'

Olivia hesitated. She could not bring herself to tell the housekeeper that she would not be returning. Besides, she could always send for the rest of her things later.

'I am not sure how long I shall stay,' she replied. 'Just a small trunk will suffice for the moment.'

'Very well, milady. I shall give the orders now.'

Olivia smiled but her eyes were shadowed by sadness as she walked from the room. She had not considered what to do with Brutus when she left Briarwood, and it would obviously not be suitable for a large dog to live in her aunt's small house at Bath. He was used to being able to roam in the countryside at will, and would feel trapped if he were prevented from running free.

She supposed he would have to be left behind as well, and she could only hope that like Jack he would forget her in time—as she must try to forget them.

Jack was frowning as he left his horse at the stables and began to walk round to the front of the house. He had meant to return sooner so that he could be present when Gransden took his leave, but his business had taken longer than he expected. His friendship with Leander Gransden had received a severe knock these past few days and he thought it might not be possible to retrieve the situation.

He would regret that, but the circumstances of his forced estrangement from Olivia had made him lose control of his emotions in a way that was foreign to him. He knew that Gransden was a hardened rake and he might have expected some show of interest in Olivia, for she was the kind of woman who would always attract other men. However, Jack was not normally a jealous man and would in other circumstances have been amused rather than angered by Gransden's obvious efforts to seduce his wife. Efforts he was well aware had gathered no reward.

He had not been quite as intoxicated as Olivia thought him the previous evening, and though his eyes were closed, his head a little unsteady, his hearing had remained unimpaired. He was well aware that Olivia had seen off Gransden's clumsy attempt to take advantage of her. Only her prompt action had prevented him from betraying his fury, though afterwards, he had seen the amusing side of the affair.

He had gone to his wife's parlour that morning to apologise, in the hope that they might find some way of salvaging at least the shreds of their marriage, but Olivia's words had nearly torn the heart out of his breast.

It was what he had been preparing for ever since he discovered his father's madness...but now that

Olivia seemed to have accepted the need for them to live apart he had discovered that he could not bear to let her go. Somehow he must find an answer to… Surely that was Heggan's carriage drawn up outside the house!

Jack's heart began to race wildly. His grandfather had come in answer to his letter. At last he would know the truth, however unpalatable that might be. He would know then what he must do to safeguard Olivia's future.

He strode into the house, waving Jenkins aside. 'Yes, I know the earl is here—in the front parlour?'

'Yes, milord.'

'Is her ladyship with him?'

'No, milord. I believe she went out.'

Jack nodded but did not stay to question Jenkins further. He was in a fever of impatience to greet his grandfather. At least there would be an end to uncertainty.

The Earl was standing by the window gazing out as Jack entered. He turned and frowned as he saw him.

'Forgive me, sir. Had I known you…'

The Earl held up his hand to stop him. 'No, Jack. It is I who should beg your pardon. I fear I have caused you much grief…'

'So it is true then?' Jack turned a ghastly shade of grey. He had hoped so much his grandfather would deny it but now he saw that the older man was deeply troubled. 'No, do not blame yourself, sir. It was my choice to marry…'

'And the best thing you have ever done, I dare say,' the Earl replied. 'You have no need to fear that you will end your days as Stanhope did, a raving lunatic. If that is what you fear, you may set your mind at rest at once.'

'Then the madness was not hereditary?' Jack could scarcely believe it. 'Was it some foul sickness that came upon him?'

'I did not say that,' replied the Earl. 'The madness was inherited from your grandmother's family. My poor Mary never suffered herself but she passed it on to her son, as did her grandmother. It was a form of sickness that was transferred through the female line but showed its worst form only in the males of the family. I believe several of her uncles and cousins inherited it, though of course I knew nothing of this until after Stanhope was born.'

Jack frowned. 'Then I am doomed to suffer the sickness later in life. I could pass it on to my son…'

'No, that is not so. You do not carry the same blood…'

'I do not understand what you are saying, sir…unless I am not Stanhope's son?' Jack's eyes narrowed as he thought he saw the answer in Heggan's eyes. 'Then my mother…was carrying me when she married Stanhope?'

'You are not the child of either Lady or Lord

Stanhope,' the Earl said and sighed heavily. 'Forgive me for keeping this from you for so many years, Jack, but it was forced upon me. Silence was the price I paid for making sure you were accepted as Lady Stanhope's child.'

Jack was bewildered. 'I fear I do not understand. If I am not their child...whose son am I?'

'Have you not guessed yet?' The Earl looked tired and ill. 'Forgive me, I must sit down. I had returned to Ireland when your letter reached me at last, having been sent on from Stanhope. I had not been well and I have travelled without rest to reach you, knowing how you must be suffering thinking yourself the child of my son.'

'Please be seated, sir. Would you care for a glass of brandy?'

'Yes, please.' The Earl placed a hand to his breast, waiting until Jack poured the brandy from a decanter on the sideboard and brought it to him. He drank it down in one go, then closed his eyes for a moment.

'If you are ill this can wait.'

'No, no,' the Earl said and opened his eyes again. 'I should have spoken years ago, but I gave my word and I have kept it. For years Stanhope did not seem to be badly afflicted by his sickness, and since he seemed not to be capable of giving his wife a child I hoped that I would never need to speak. Now, I must do so. You are my son, Jack, not Stanhope's, the child of my autumn years. You may forget your fears, there has never been a shred of insanity in my family I promise you.'

'Your son?' The colour left Jack's face. 'But not Lady Heggan's?'

'No, not poor Mary's,' the Earl said, and a tear issued from the corner of his eye. 'After Stanhope was born she told me the truth and begged that I would never visit her bed again. Her fear that her son would develop the illness made her an invalid. Your mother was a gentle girl, Jack. Helen was not beautiful, but she was generous and sweet, and she gave me a great deal of happiness. She came of good birth, from a family that had been reduced to poverty by gambling. I employed her to be a companion to my wife, but in the end she became so much more. I loved her desperately, you see, and when she died some hours after your birth I vowed that her son should inherit all I had to give.'

'But I am a bastard,' Jack said. 'If Stanhope had had a son…'

'By this time I had learned that he was blaming Lady Stanhope for being barren,' the Earl said. 'I believe he may have treated her badly, Jack, though she has never complained to me.'

'I once saw him rape and beat her,' Jack said. 'I was a child and could do nothing to stop him. I thought she blamed me for letting him hurt her. I thought it was the reason she seemed to turn against me, to shut me out of her life.'

'She desperately wanted a child when I struck my bargain with her,' the Earl said. 'I thought it the natural desire of a woman for a baby, but perhaps she thought it would keep Stanhope from her bed. She made me promise I would never interfere in your life, that no one should ever know you were not truly her child.'

'But how was she able to deceive Stanhope? To make the world believe I was hers?'

'She was often alone at Stanhope in those days. Six months had passed since her husband had visited her. She was always quite a large woman. We brought in a midwife who declared her with child, and we smuggled you into the bedchamber. Lady Stanhope screamed a great deal and the servants were kept from the room. I believe there are some women who show no signs of being with child, others who have given birth without ever knowing they had conceived until the last.' The Earl paused for breath. 'Besides, she had few friends, no one she might have confided in. Her mother was dead, though her father visited her sometimes. Sir Joshua may have suspected something, indeed I have often thought he may have suspected the truth. However, he never gave any sign that he was anything other than your grandfather.'

'He always loved me,' Jack said and frowned. 'I would not like to think he was deceived.'

'You are thinking of the fortune he left you. Rest

easy, Jack. He had no one else he loved so well as you.'

'Then I am truly your son?' Jack could still hardly believe it, but he was beginning to realise that a black cloud had been lifted from his life. 'I cannot pass on Stanhope's madness to my son?'

'No one can predict the future with certainty, but you have as much chance as any man of giving your wife healthy children.'

'No one can predict the future with certainty...' Jack nodded. 'Olivia said something similar to me.'

'She is a sensible woman besides being a beauty. You were lucky to find her, Jack.'

'Yes, I know.'

'I hope you have not distressed your wife with this nonsense,' the Earl said and frowned as saw the answer in Jack's face. 'You had better go and find her, put her mind at ease.'

'Yes...Father.' Jack was suddenly overcome with emotion. He went to kneel by the Earl's side, taking the frail hand in his own. 'You have worn yourself out to come and tell me this, sir. I can never express my gratitude sufficiently.'

'Stuff and nonsense!' said the Earl stoutly. 'I am a little tired at the moment, but I dare say I shall live long enough to see my first grandchild. Off with you and find that lovely girl you married. When you have told her all she needs to know, you may bring her to me. I have wanted to tell her she reminds me of my

Helen. It is just a look when she smiles, no more, but it is there.'

'I shall bring her to you soon,' Jack promised and kissed his hand. 'I am glad you have told me the truth at last. Perhaps we can make up for all the lost years.'

'Perhaps,' the Earl said in a gruff tone. 'Whatever else you think of me, Jack, believe that I always loved you. I wished a thousand times I had not given you to the Stanhopes, but to have taken you back would have deprived you of your birthright.'

'Titles mean very little, sir,' Jack said. 'It is the people who love you who matter.'

'Then waste no more time in bringing that girl back to me!'

'I shall find Olivia now,' Jack promised as he rose to his feet. 'God bless and keep you, Father. You have given me the greatest gift possible.'

The Earl nodded, leaning his head back against the chair as his son went hurriedly from the room. He had been in time, which was all that mattered now. Jack's happiness was secured and if death claimed him now, he was ready. Yet he would pray to be spared long enough to see Jack's child in the arms of that beautiful girl he had married.

Jack felt as if he walked with winged feet as he left the parlour and ran upstairs to his wife's room. He was free at last to show Olivia just how much he adored her, free to hold her and kiss her—to take her to his bed whenever they both wished for it. The shadows which had lain over for him for so many years had gone, melted away like the morning mist. All his life he had known that Stanhope hated him, sensed that his mother did not truly love him, though she had often been kind when he was small. It was only as he grew to manhood that she had become cold towards him. Yet how could he blame her after the life she must have lived?

Jack sensed that the man he had believed to be his father had suspected his wife of betraying him with another man. Stanhope had never in later years given her a child; he had accused her of being barren before Jack was born. Did he afterwards think he himself was sterile and therefore that his wife must be a whore?

It did not excuse his behaviour towards her, but it explained why he had come to hate both her and Jack. As his madness closed in on him, he had lost touch with right and wrong, becoming the monster Jack had so despised. Yet now he could find it in his heart to pity Stanhope.

'My wife?' Jack asked as he entered her bedchamber and found the maid packing her clothes. 'Where may I find her, please?'

'I do not know, sir,' Rosie replied. 'I believe she went out earlier—when Viscount Gransden left this afternoon…'

Jack's heart jerked with pain. Olivia had left at the same time as Gransden? She had gone with him! He had driven her away with his jealousy and his unkindness. He was too late! He loved her so much and she had gone.

'I think it was to the stables,' Rosie went on, unaware of the anguish she had momentarily caused her master. 'To see that great brute of a dog, I believe.'

'To the stables? Thank God!' Jack cried, startling the maid. His eyes narrowed as he realised what she was doing. 'Why are you packing her things?'

'Mrs Jenkins told me to pack one small trunk,' Rosie said, feeling scared by his furious expression. 'Her ladyship is to accompany Lady Burton home, sir.'

'Ah yes, of course,' Jack said and nodded. 'I remember she mentioned something of the kind.'

He turned and walked from the room, hurrying back down the stairs and out of the house. The fear that she might have gone, that he might have lost her, was still with him, but then he saw her walking from the direction of the temple with Brutus at her heels.

'Olivia,' he cried and hurried towards her. 'I wondered where you were. I was anxious. You have not been to the woods again?'

'No—though I have been told the gypsies have gone.'

'Yes. I doubt they will return,' Jack said. He did not wish to tell her that the man who had attacked her would never be able to return, nor that they had found him dead of his wounds. Olivia would find that horrifying and he did not want her to become afraid of the faithful dog that had killed for her sake. 'But you must still take Brutus with you whenever you walk there. You will promise me?'

'Yes, I promise.' Had he forgotten that they had agreed she should go away? Olivia's heart began to beat wildly as she saw the look in his eyes—a look she had not seen since he was courting her at Camberwell. 'I had to take Brutus for a walk. He was missing me.'

'I have missed you, Olivia,' Jack said. He took a step towards her, his eyes beseeching her not to turn away. 'I love you so much, my darling. Forgive me for the pain and hurt I have caused you since our wedding. I beg you to love me, and believe that I shall never willingly hurt you again.'

'You did not do so willingly this time,' she whispered, her throat tight with emotion. A shiver of pleasure went through her as he trailed his fingers lovingly down her cheek. 'What has happened, Jack? Something has changed. You are no longer afraid to touch me.'

'I was afraid only for your sake,' he said huskily. 'Afraid that my touch would defile you, destroy your loveliness.'

'I never thought that,' Olivia said. 'You are not insane, Jack. Even if your father was at the end of his life, you are not touched by his sickness.'

'No, his sickness cannot touch me,' Jack said, 'because I am not his son. I am the natural son of the Earl of Heggan—not his grandson. The madness came from Lady Heggan's family and since I do not carry her blood, I am free of it. My mother was a gentle, sweet girl of good family who was employed to be her companion.'

'Oh; Jack...' Tears filled Olivia's eyes. 'Oh, my darling! I know how much this means to you...to us both.'

'Then you can forgive me for my jealousy and my unkindness to you, Olivia? I have not killed your love?'

'How could you ever think that?' she asked, then nodded as she gazed up into his eyes and understood his unspoken fear. 'I was leaving for your sake, Jack. After I saw what I had done to you. You had drunk too much wine to help you forget. I knew that as the empty years went by you would grow to hate me, and I thought it better we should part.'

'I could never hate you, Olivia. You are all I have ever dreamed of—and at last I have learned how to love. I thought I would never feel true love. Passion, affection for friends, yes, I have known them in the past—but never the kind of love I feel for you. I would rather die than live without you, my darling.'

'Then you shall live until we are both old,' she said, a teasing light in her lovely eyes. 'For I do not intend to leave you, Jack. Not ever.'

'As long as you promise to return I can bear it,' he

said. 'Lady Burton will expect you to keep your promise to see her home, dearest.'

'Yes, but she would be even happier if you were to accompany us,' Olivia told him. 'She likes you, Jack. She told me she was happy that we had found each other.'

'The compliment is returned,' Jack replied, his eyes intent on her face. 'I wondered if you were wise to invite her here, Olivia, but after observing you together, I have seen the affection between you. We shall certainly accompany your aunt to her home and stay with her for a few days. You might like to go out in company and see your friends?'

'Yes, that would be pleasant,' Olivia said. 'But I should be just as happy here. Besides, you have not forgotten that you promised me a trip to Italy?'

Her lovely eyes were alight with wickedness. Jack slipped his arm about her waist as they began to walk back to the house together.

'No, I have not forgotten,' he said. 'If it is your wish we shall travel abroad this autumn. You have only to tell me what you wish for, my darling, and it shall be yours.'

'Then you mean to spoil me?' She tilted her head at him. 'I was a very spoiled child, you know. I had begun to improve my character, but I shall soon slip into my old ways. I think you would do better to beat me, Jack.'

'Oh, no,' he said softly and drew her to him, both

arms about her waist. 'That is one thing I shall never do, my darling.'

Olivia lifted her face for his kiss. Her heart was beginning to sing as his mouth came down to take gentle possession of hers. She had never imagined that he would deliberately hurt her in any way. These past weeks had revealed his nature to her and she knew what a loving, thoughtful man he truly was.

'Then I must resign myself to being spoiled,' she said, giving him a wicked smile. 'In which case you will not refuse to let me take Brutus with me when we travel?'

'That brute?' Jack turned his head to look at the dog, who was watching them with interest. 'You do not expect me to share a carriage with him, I hope?'

'Oh, no, he may travel with the luggage and my maid, though not Rosie. She doesn't like him. I shall ask one of the others to accompany us.'

'And leave poor Rosie behind?' Jack raised his brows. 'I think she may sooner grow fonder of Brutus rather than be left behind.'

'Then I may take him?'

'Would he allow us to go without him?' Jack chuckled. It was a delightful sound and one that Olivia had seldom heard from him. 'But if you or he imagine that he is going to share our bedchamber you are both much mistaken.'

'I dare say he will not mind that so very much,' Olivia said. 'Providing we leave him a nice juicy bone.' She reached up and kissed him on the mouth. 'And now, my love, I think we should go in before all the servants stop work and come to watch the spectacle of their master making love to his wife in the garden.'

Jack laughed out loud as he saw that several pairs of interested eyes were already turned in their direction.

'Anyone would think they have nothing better to do,' he said in a voice that carried to the gardeners. 'Clearly I employ too many people.'

Olivia giggled as the men went instantly back to work. She smiled at Jack and they walked into the house, their arms about each other.

Jack lay on the bed, watching as Olivia sat brushing her hair. They had been married for nearly three months and were at home again after a visit to Ireland, where they had seen the Earl comfortably settled in his home.

'Well, my love, when shall we think about leaving for Italy?' Jack asked, reaching out to scratch Brutus behind the ears. 'Shall I set the arrangements in hand?'

Olivia placed her brush back on top of the dressing-table and turned to look at him. She hesitated for a moment, then got to her feet and walked to the bed, shifting Brutus a few inches to make room next to Jack.

'You should not indulge him so,' she scolded, her eyes alight with mischief.

'He takes no notice of me these days. He will only go to his own bed when you tell him.'

Olivia gurgled with laughter. 'Oh, my poor Jack,' she murmured and bent to kiss him on the lips. 'Shall you mind very much if we postpone our trip? Only Beatrice wants us to go to her at Ravensden for Christmas.'

'I care not where we are as long as I have you.' He raised his brows. 'I thought you wanted to travel?'

'Perhaps one day,' Olivia agreed. 'But I think it might not be wise just yet…' She smiled at him lovingly. 'You see, I believe I may be carrying the child your father longs for so much.'

'My child?' Jack sat up suddenly, causing Brutus to look at him reproachfully. 'Truly, Olivia?'

'Does that please you, Jack?'

'You know the answer,' he replied, reaching out to touch her cheek. 'Of course I want our child—but it is a little soon. Do you mind?'

'I am very happy,' she said and tossed back her hair. She traced the line of his mouth with her finger. 'I think it may have happened that first afternoon…'

'Thank God we did not know it before my father told me the truth,' Jack said and drew her close to him.

Olivia responded to his embrace, then got to her feet.

'Come, Brutus,' she said, opening the door to the dressing-room. 'Time for your own bed.'

Brutus obeyed instantly, licking the hand she used to give him his last caress of the day, then went into the dressing-room.

Olivia closed the door and returned to her husband's arms.